PUFFIN BOOKS

# THE
# FOREST OF DOOM

Only the foolhardy or the very brave would willingly risk a journey into Darkwood Forest, where strange, twisting paths wind their way into the eerie depths. who knows what monstrous creatures lurk in the threatening shadows, or what deadly adventures await the unwary traveller? Do YOU dare to enter?

In a desperate race against time, deep within Darkwood, your quest is to find the missing pieces of the legendary Hammer of Stonebridge, which was fashioned by Dwarfs to protect peaceful Stonebridge against its ancient doom.

Two dice, a pencil and an eraser are all you need to embark on this thrilling adventure of sword and sorcery, complete with its elaborate combat system and a score sheet to record your gains and losses.

Many dangers lie ahead and your success is by no means certain. It's up to YOU to decide which paths to take, which dangers to risk and which adversaries to fight!

Ian Livingstone is a co-founder (with Steve Jackson) of the highly successful Games Workshop chain.

## Fighting Fantasy Gamebooks

FIGHTING FANTASY – The Introductory Role-Playing Game
THE RIDDLING REAVER – Four thrilling adventures
THE TROLLTOOTH WARS – A Fighting Fantasy Novel

**The Advanced Fighting Fantasy System**
OUT OF THE PIT: Fighting Fantasy Monsters
TITAN: The Fighting Fantasy World
DUNGEONEER – An Introduction to the World of Role–Playing Games

# Ian Livingstone

# THE FOREST OF DOOM

*Illustrated by Malcolm Barter*

**Puffin Books**

## PUFFIN BOOKS

Published by the Penguin Group
Penguin Books Ltd, 27 Wrights Lane, London W8 5TZ, England
Penguin Books USA Inc., 375 Hudson Street, New York, New York 10014, USA
Penguin Books Australia Ltd, Ringwood, Victoria, Australia
Penguin Books Canada Ltd, 2801 John Street, Markham, Ontario, Canada L3R 1B4
Penguin Books (NZ) Ltd, 182–190 Wairau Road, Auckland 10, New Zealand

Penguin Books Ltd, Registered Offices: Harmondsworth, Middlesex, England

First published 1983
29  30  28

Printed in England by Clays Ltd, St Ives plc
Set in Linotron Palatino

For Liz and Carol

# CONTENTS

# HOW TO FIGHT THE CREATURES
## OF DARKWOOD FOREST

Before embarking on your adventure, you must first determine your own strengths and weaknesses. You have in your possession a sword and a backpack containing provisions (food and drink) for the trip. You have been preparing for your quest by training yourself in swordplay and exercising vigorously to build up your stamina.

To see how effective your preparations have been, you must use the dice to determine your initial SKILL and STAMINA scores. On pages 16–19 there is an *Adventure Sheet* which you may use to record the details of an adventure. On it you will find boxes for recording your SKILL and STAMINA scores.

You are advised to either record your scores on the *Adventure Sheet* in pencil, or make photocopies of the page to use in future adventures.

### Skill, Stamina and Luck

Roll one die. Add 6 to this number and enter this total in the SKILL box on the *Adventure Sheet*.

Roll both dice. Add 12 to the number rolled and enter this total in the STAMINA box.

There is also a LUCK box. Roll one die, add 6 to this number and enter this total in the LUCK box.

For reasons that will be explained below, SKILL, STAMINA and LUCK scores change constantly during an adventure. You must keep an accurate record of these scores and for this reason you are advised either to write small in the boxes or to keep an eraser handy. But never rub out your *Initial* scores. Although you may be awarded additional SKILL, STAMINA and LUCK points, these totals may never exceed your *Initial* scores, except on very rare occasions, when you will be instructed on a particular page.

Your SKILL score reflects your swordsmanship and general fighting expertise; the higher the better. Your STAMINA score reflects your general constitution, your will to survive, your determination and overall fitness; the higher your STAMINA score, the longer you will be able to survive. Your LUCK score indicates how naturally lucky a person you are. Luck – and magic – are facts of life in the fantasy kingdom you are about to explore.

## Battles

You will often come across pages in the book which instruct you to fight a creature of some sort. An option to flee may be given, but if not – or if you choose to attack the creature anyway – you must resolve the battle as described below.

First record the creature's SKILL and STAMINA scores in the first vacant Monster Encounter Box on your *Adventure Sheet*. The scores for each creature are given in the book each time you have an encounter.

The sequence of combat is then:

1. Roll both dice once for the creature. Add its SKILL score. This total is the creature's Attack Strength.
2. Roll both dice once for yourself. Add the number rolled to your current SKILL score. This total is your Attack Strength.
3. If your Attack Strength is higher than that of the creature, you have wounded it. Proceed to step 4. If the creature's Attack Strength is higher than yours, it has wounded you. Proceed to step 5. If both Attack Strength totals are the same, you have avoided each other's blows – start the next Attack Round from step 1 above.
4. You have wounded the creature, so subtract 2 points from its STAMINA score. You may use your LUCK here to do additional damage (see over).
5. The creature has wounded you, so subtract 2 points from your own STAMINA score. Again you may use LUCK at this stage (see over).
6. Make the appropriate adjustments to either the creature's or your own STAMINA scores (and your LUCK score if you used LUCK – see over).
7. Begin the next Attack Round by returning to your current SKILL score and repeating steps 1–6. This sequence continues until the STAMINA score of either you or the creature you are fighting has been reduced to zero (death).

## Escaping

On some pages you may be given the option of running away from a battle should things be going badly for you. However, if you do run away, the creature automatically gets in one wound on you (subtract 2 STAMINA points) as you flee. Such is the price of cowardice. Note that you may use LUCK on this wound in the normal way (see below). You may only *Escape* if that option is specifically given to you on the page.

## Fighting More Than One Creature

If you come across more than one creature in a particular encounter, the instructions on that page will tell you how to handle the battle. Sometimes you will treat them as a single monster; sometimes you will fight each one in turn.

## Luck

At various times during your adventure, either in battles or when you come across situations in which you could either be lucky or unlucky (details of these are given on the pages themselves), you may call on your luck to make the outcome more favourable. But beware! Using luck is a risky business and if you are *un*lucky, the results could be disastrous.

The procedure for using your luck is as follows: roll two dice. If the number rolled is equal to or less than your current LUCK score, you have been lucky and the result will go in your favour. If the number rolled is higher than your current LUCK score, you have been unlucky and you will be penalized.

This procedure is known as *Testing your Luck*. Each time you *Test your Luck*, you must subtract one point from your current LUCK score. Thus you will soon realize that the more you rely on your luck, the more risky this will become.

*Using Luck in Battles*

On certain pages of the book you will be told to *Test your Luck* and will be told the consequences of your being lucky or unlucky. However, in battles, you always have the option of using your luck either to inflict a more serious wound on a creature you have just wounded, or to minimize the effects of a wound the creature has just inflicted on you.

If you have just wounded the creature, you may *Test your Luck* as described above. If you are lucky, you have inflicted a severe wound and may subtract an *extra* 2 points from the creature's STAMINA score. However, if you are unlucky, the wound was a mere graze and you must restore 1 point to the creature's STAMINA (i.e. instead of scoring the normal 2 points of damage, you have now scored only 1).

If the creature has just wounded you, you may *Test your Luck* to try to minimize the wound. If you are lucky, you have managed to avoid the full damage of the blow. Restore 1 point of STAMINA (i.e. instead of doing 2 points of damage it has done only 1). If you are unlucky, you have taken a more serious blow. Subtract 1 extra STAMINA point.

Remember that you must subtract 1 point from your own LUCK score each time you *Test your Luck*.

## Restoring Skill, Stamina and Luck

### *Skill*

Your SKILL score will not change much during your adventure. Occasionally, a page may give instructions to increase or decrease your SKILL score. A Magic Weapon may increase your SKILL, but remember that only one weapon can be used at a time! You cannot claim 2 SKILL bonuses for carrying two Magic Swords. Your SKILL score can never exceed its *Initial* value unless specifically instructed. Drinking the Potion of Skill (see later) will restore your SKILL to its *Initial* level at any time.

### *Stamina and Provisions*

Your STAMINA score will change a lot during your adventure as you fight monsters and undertake arduous tasks. As you near your goal, your STAMINA level may be dangerously low and battles may be particularly risky, so be careful!

Your backpack contains enough Provisions for ten meals. You may rest and eat at any time except when engaged in a Battle. Eating a meal restores 4 STAMINA points. When you eat a meal, add 4 points to your STAMINA score and deduct 1 point from your Provisions. A separate Provisions Remaining box is provided on the *Adventure Sheet* for recording details of Provisions. Remember that you have a long way to go, so use your Provisions wisely!

Remember also that your STAMINA score may never exceed its *Initial* value unless specifically instructed on a page. Drinking the Potion of Strength (see later) will restore your STAMINA to its *Initial* level at any time.

### Luck

Additions to your LUCK score are awarded through the adventure when you have been particularly lucky. Details are given on the pages of the book. Remember that, as with SKILL and STAMINA, your LUCK score may never exceed its *Initial* value unless specifically instructed on a page. Drinking the Potion of Fortune (see later) will restore your LUCK to its *Initial* level at any time, and increase your *Initial* LUCK by 1 point.

# EQUIPMENT AND POTIONS

You will start your adventure with a bare minimum of equipment, but you may find or buy other items during your travels. You are armed with a sword and are dressed in leather armour. You have a backpack to hold your Provisions and any treasures you may come across.

In addition, you may take one bottle of a magical potion which will aid you on your quest. You may choose to take a bottle of any of the following:

A Potion of Skill – restores SKILL points
A Potion of Strength – restores STAMINA points
A Potion of Fortune – restores LUCK points and adds 1 to *Initial* LUCK

These potions may be taken at any time during your adventure (except when engaged in a Battle). Taking a measure of potion will restore SKILL, STAMINA or LUCK scores to their *Initial* level (and the Potion of Fortune will add 1 point to your *Initial* LUCK score before LUCK is restored).

Each bottle of potion contains enough for *one* measure, i.e. the characteristic may be restored once during an adventure. Make a note on your *Adventure Sheet* when you have used up a potion.

Remember also that you may only choose *one* of the three potions to take on your trip, so choose wisely!

# HINTS ON PLAY

There is one true way through Darkwood Forest and it will take you several attempts to find it. Make notes and draw a map as you explore – this map will be invaluable in future adventures and enable you to progress rapidly through to unexplored sections.

Not all areas contain treasure; many merely contain traps and creatures which you will no doubt fall foul of. There are many 'wild goose chase' passages and while you may indeed progress through to your ultimate destination, it is by no means certain that you will find what you are searching for.

It will be realized that entries make no sense if read in numerical order. It is essential that you read only the entries you are instructed to read. Reading other entries will only cause confusion and may lessen the excitement during play.

The one true way involves a minimum of risk and any player, no matter how weak on initial dice rolls, should be able to get through fairly easily.

May the luck of the gods go with you on the adventure ahead!

# ADVENTURE SHEET

| SKILL | STAMINA | LUCK |
|-------|---------|------|
| *Initial* | *Initial* | *Initial* |
| *Skill* = 6 | *Stamina* = 5 | *Luck* = 1 |
| 5 | -3, 7 | |
| | -4, -1 | |

| EQUIPMENT LIST | GOLD |
|----------------|------|
| map | 30, 29, |
| wistle | 31  36 |

**JEWELS**

**POTIONS**

**PROVISIONS REMAINING**

# MONSTER ENCOUNTER BOXES

| | | |
|---|---|---|
| *Skill=*<br>*Stamina=* | *Skill=*<br>*Stamina=* | *Skill=*<br>*Stamina=* |
| *Skill=*<br>*Stamina=* | *Skill=*<br>*Stamina=* | *Skill=*<br>*Stamina=* |
| *Skill=*<br>*Stamina=* | *Skill=*<br>*Stamina=* | *Skill=*<br>*Stamina=* |
| *Skill=*<br>*Stamina=* | *Skill=*<br>*Stamina=* | *Skill=*<br>*Stamina=* |

# BACKGROUND

You are an adventurer, a sword for hire, and have been roaming the northern borderlands of your kingdom. Having always spurned the dullness of village life, you now wander the lands in search of wealth and danger. Despite the long walks and rough outdoor life you are content with your unknown destiny. The world holds no fears for you as you are a skilful warrior, well practised in the art of slaying evil men and beasts with your trusty sword. Not once during the last ten days since entering the northern borderlands have you set eyes upon another person. This does not worry you at all, as you are happy with your own company and enjoy the slow, sunny days hunting, eating and sleeping.

It is evening, and having feasted on a dinner of rabbit, spit-roasted on an open fire, you settle down to sleep beneath your sheepskin blanket. There's a full moon, and the light sparkles on the blade of your broadsword skewered into the ground by your side. You gaze at it, wondering when you will next have to wipe the blood of some vile creature from its sharp edge. These are strange lands, inhabited by weird and loathsome beasts – goblins, trolls and even dragons.

As the flame of your camp fire gently dies, you

begin to drift asleep, and images of screaming, green-faced trolls flicker through your mind. Suddenly, in the bushes to your left, you hear the loud crack of a twig breaking under a clumsy foot. You leap up and grab your sword from the ground. You stand motionless but alert, ready to pounce on your unseen adversary. Then you hear a groan, followed by the dull thud of a body falling to the ground. Is it a trap? Slowly you walk over to the bush where the noise is coming from and carefully pull back the branches. You look down to see a little old man with a great bushy beard, his face contorted with pain. You crouch down to remove the iron helmet covering his balding head and notice two crossbow bolts protruding from the stomach of his plump, chain-mail-clad torso. Picking him up, you carry him over to the fire and stir the dying embers into life. After covering him with the sheepskin blanket, you manage to get the old man to drink a little water. He coughs and moans. He sits up rigid, eyes staring fixedly ahead, and starts to shout.

'I'll get them! I'll get them! Don't you fear, Gillibran, Bigleg is coming to bring you the hammer. Oh yes, indeed I am. Oh yes. . .'

The dwarf, whose name you presume to be Bigleg, is obviously delirious from the poison-tipped bolts lodged in his stomach. You watch as he slumps down again to the ground, then whisper his name in his ear. His eyes stare unblinkingly at you, as he again starts to shout.

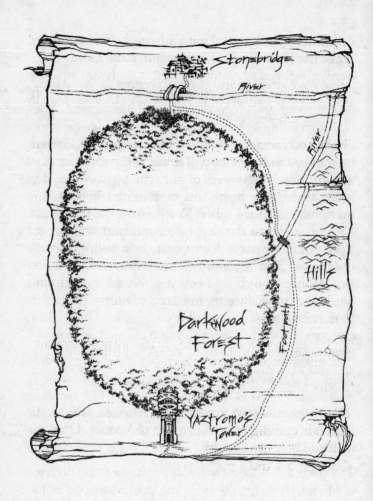

'Ambush! Look out! Ambush! Aagh! The hammer! Take the hammer to Gillibran! Save the dwarfs!'

His eyes half close and the pain seems to ease a little, and as the delirium subsides, he speaks to you again in a low whisper.

'Help us, friend . . . take the hammer to Gillibran . . . only the hammer will unite our people against the trolls. . . We were on our way to Darkwood in search of the hammer . . . ambushed by the little people . . . others killed . . . the map in my pouch will take you to the home of Yaztromo, the master mage of these parts . . . he has great magics for sale to protect you against the creatures of Darkwood . . . take my gold . . . I beg you to find the hammer and take it to Gillibran, my Lord of Stonebridge . . . you will be well rewarded. . .'

Bigleg opens his mouth to start another sentence, but nothing comes out except his last dying breath. You sit down and ponder Bigleg's words. Who is Gillibran? Who is Yaztromo? What is all the fuss about the dwarfish hammer? You reach over to the still body of Bigleg and remove the pouch from the leather belt around his waist. Inside you find 30 Gold Pieces and a map (*opposite*).

Jingling the coins in your hand you think of the possible rewards which may await you just for returning a hammer to a village of dwarfs. You decide to try to find the hammer in Darkwood Forest; it's been a few weeks since your last good battle, and, what is more, you are likely to be well paid for this one.

With your mind made up, you settle down to sleep, having taken back the sheepskin blanket from poor Bigleg. In the morning you bury the old dwarf and gather up your possessions. You examine the map, look up to the sun, and find your bearings. Whistling merrily, you head off south at a good pace, eager to meet this man Yaztromo and see what he has to offer.

# NOW TURN OVER

**1** *The tower is set back on the edge of Darkwood, some fifty metres away from the path.*

Your walk to Yaztromo's takes a little over half a day, and you arrive at his stone tower home dirty and hungry. As the tower is set back on the edges of Darkwood some fifty metres away from the path you have been following, it is difficult to find. Finally you walk up to the huge oak door, somewhat relieved to find that it does exist and that Bigleg had not been speaking wildly in his delirium. A large brass bell and gong hang from the stone archway. As you ring the bell, a shiver runs down your spine and you realize that the loud 'bong' invades a deep silence, which you had not noticed before. There are no sounds of birds or animals to be heard. You wait anxiously at the door and hear slow footsteps descending stairs from the tower above. A small wooden slot in the door slides open, and two eyes appear and examine you.

'Well, who are you?' demands a grumpy voice through the hole.

You answer that you are an adventurer in search of the master mage Yaztromo, intending to purchase magical items from him to combat the creatures of Darkwood Forest.

'Oh! Well in that case, if you are interested in buying some of my merchandise, you had better come up. I am Yaztromo.'

He then turns and slowly climbs the stone stairs. Will you:

| | |
|---|---|
| Follow him up the stairs? | Turn to **261** |
| Draw your sword and attack him? | Turn to **54** |

## 2

Your adventure ends here as your tasty fresh flesh is about to become a savoury feast for the victorious Ghoul.

## 3

You follow five more arrows to the trunk of an old dead tree still rooted in the ground. You see that the trunk is hollow and that the hole continues through the trunk into the ground to make a tunnel. It is dark down the hole and you cannot see how far it is to the bottom. Do you have a Ring of Light? If you do, turn to **322**. If you do not possess this item, turn to **120**.

## 4

Lose 4 STAMINA points. If you are still alive you manage to pull the arrow from your shoulder although the pain is agonizing. If you still wish to enter the cave, turn to **49**. If you wish to crawl back to the junction, turn to **93**.

## 5

Sitting in the ornate throne you feel strangely uncomfortable. The two Clone Warriors grovel on the floor in front of you in complete subservience. Do they expect you to become their new master? If you wish to place the gold crown on your head, turn to **333**. If you wish to leave the alcove and climb up the rest of the steps to the roof of the cavern, turn to **249**.

### 6

As you walk past the Goblin he growls unlike anything you have ever heard before, a growl that you would not expect a Goblin to make. Feeling a little nervous you head quickly north. Turn to **148**.

### 7

You draw your sword and prepare to meet the yellow- and black-striped attackers. They are KILLER BEES and will attack in separate droves, each drove counting as a single creature.

|                   | SKILL | STAMINA |
|-------------------|-------|---------|
| First KILLER BEES  | 7     | 3       |
| Second KILLER BEES | 8     | 4       |
| Third KILLER BEES  | 7     | 4       |

If you win, turn to **23**.

### 8

Walking along the path, you hear footsteps and arguing voices ahead of you. If you wish to meet their owners, turn to **317**. If you would rather hide in the bushes to let them walk by, turn to **392**.

### 9

You unlock the door and step back, drawing your sword in case the Goblin tries to attack you. He picks up a wooden stool and, waving it in the air, kicks the door open and charges at you screaming. You must fight.

GOBLIN            SKILL 5            STAMINA 4

If you win, turn to **176**.

## 10

You pick up a good-sized rock off the floor and take aim. You throw the rock with all your might at the Ogre but are dismayed to see it fly past his head and crash against the far wall of the cave. You curse, but decide nevertheless to rush into the cave to attack the Ogre (turn to **290**).

## 11

You start to lose your balance as the illusion distorts your mind. You close your eyes and hold your head in your hands but it makes no difference. You reel around the room and then fall to the floor unconscious. Turn to **353**.

## 12

You tell the Gnome that perhaps you had been a little hasty in drawing your sword, but you had to be prepared for anything within the evil boundary of Darkwood Forest. He replies that that is no excuse for drawing your weapon on a defenceless old man and, if you want your sword back, it will cost you 10 Gold Pieces or two items of treasure from your backpack. You pay him what you will and, to your relief, your beloved sword is returned. If you wish to continue the conversation with him, turn to **271**.

If you have had enough of the Gnome and would rather head west along the path, turn to **67**.

## 13

The vibrations feel like shock waves which seem to hammer your body. Your legs feel like lead and you are unable to move them. Suddenly the hut collapses and crashes to the ground. The sky darkens and a wind starts to howl all about you. The wind blows harder and becomes as strong as a gale, its force knocking you to the ground. You cling to the porch and shield your face from the dirt and debris thrown up by the gale. Above the deafening noise of the wind you hear laughter followed by a deep voice rejoicing, 'I'm free! I'm free!' You have released an EARTH ELEMENTAL on to the world – lose 3 LUCK points. Gradually the howling wind dies down and the skies brighten. You pick yourself up from out of the rubble and walk slowly back to the path to head north again. Turn to **149**.

## 14

The pit is circular with smooth sides and you are too weak from your fall to climb out. You call for help, but nobody comes to your aid. You sit down and ponder your fate. After about an hour you hear a noise overhead. You look up to see the bearded face of a stocky man wearing a fur hat. He looks annoyed. He is a fur trapper and you have ruined his trap. He shouts down to you that if you expect him to throw a rope down to rescue you, it is going to cost you 3 Gold Pieces. Failing that, he will take

**15** *You see the shiny tip of the poison barb of a huge Sting Worm coming straight at you.*

any magical item you care to give him from your backpack. After you agree to pay off the angry fur trapper he throws down a rope to you and you climb out of the pit. You hand over the fee, crossing it off your Equipment List, and glare at the unfriendly fur trapper before setting off north again down the gorge. Turn to **255**.

## 15

The slope is steep and you slip on the slime, tumbling head over heels down the hole to the bottom, into a large earthen cavern. You jump to your feet and are alarmed to see the shiny tip of a poison barb on the tail end of a huge STING WORM coming straight at you. The Sting Worm is about five metres long and has huge yellow segments, but all you care about is protecting yourself from the barb. There is no time to scramble out of the hole – you must draw your sword and fight.

STING WORM          SKILL 8          STAMINA 7

If you win, turn to **217**.

## 16

You shout at the three humanoids who are tending a patch of red-topped fungi. Again they ignore you, continuing with their work. You take hold of a fungus top, breaking a piece off, and start to eat. It tastes good but a terrible pain grips your stomach. The fungus is poisonous. Do you have a Potion of Anti-Poison? If you do, turn to **211**. If you do not have this potion, turn to **345**.

## 17

A ladder runs down the inside of the well to the water below. However, there appears to be a tunnel just above the surface of the water, running north. It is circular and has a diameter of one metre. You may:

| | |
|---|---|
| Toss a Gold Piece into the well to make a wish | Turn to 89 |
| Descend the ladder to look down the tunnel | Turn to 256 |
| Return to the path to head west | Turn to 238 |

## 18

Your plan works and the fever dies down. Mercifully the hair on the back of your hands disappears and you slump back to sleep again, exhausted. In the morning you collect your belongings and head north along the path into the hills. Turn to 198.

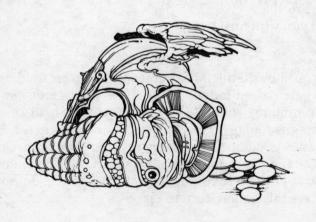

### 19

Although weak from the fever, you manage to sit up. You take hold of your sword and, gritting your teeth, cut yourself where the Werewolf bit you. Blood runs quickly from the wound, and, hopefully, the disease with it. Lose 1 STAMINA point due to loss of blood. If you are still alive, turn to **18**.

### 20

Walking east you come across a branch in the path heading south. You decide to ignore it and continue east. Turn to **277**.

### 21

The pain increases and you quickly reach into your backpack to pull out the small bottle labelled Potion of Anti-Poison. You gulp down its contents. Your body relaxes and the effects of the poison wear away. You ponder what else might be in store for you in this forest and turn north up the path. Turn to **226**.

## 22

The gas is toxic and your eyes start to water. You cough and hold your breath, running round the cave trying to escape from the gas cloud which envelops your face. Your lungs feel as though they are bursting and you are forced to inhale. Reduce your SKILL by 2 and your STAMINA by the amount of one die roll. If you are still alive, you are relieved to see the gas cloud fade away. You put the silver box in your backpack and leave the cave immediately to continue your quest northwards. Turn to 358.

## 23

You wipe the sweat from your forehead and wonder what else these evil lands have in store for you. You sit down and rest for a while. Later you set off towards the sound of the flowing water. Turn to 339.

## 24

The muscles in your neck start to stiffen and you feel the effects of poison from the darts running through your body. You reach quickly into your backpack and pull out the small bottle labelled Potion of Anti-Poison and gulp down its contents. Your body relaxes and the effects of the poison wear away. On seeing this, the Pygmies turn and run off into the grasses. Will you:

Draw your sword and run into the
grass after the Pygmies?                Turn to 377
Continue north along the path?         Turn to  92

## 25

Eventually the path levels out and you find yourself on a valley floor. The path continues north but also a new path leads off to the west.

To continue north                    Turn to 369
To go west                           Turn to  56

## 26

You decide to start your search at the wooden shelves. All the books are written in a language unfamiliar to you and contain strange diagrams. The charts and scrolls are also unintelligible to you. You open cupboards and drawers but all you find are more books, leather-bound and dusty. You are about to give up searching the room when you notice one more book on the floor, acting as a support for a broken table leg. Will you:

Pick up the book?                    Turn to 91

Give up your search and return
   to the path to head north?         Turn to 220

## 27

Wiping the thick green sap-blood from your sword you set off north again. You are relieved to see that the trees are at last beginning to thin out and appear less threatening. Turn to 329.

## 28

If you possess an Armband of Strength, turn to 52. If you do not possess this item, turn to 266.

**29** *In a small clearing amidst the trees you see two small creatures with warty skin.*

## 29

In a small clearing amidst the trees you see two small creatures with warty skin, dressed in leather armour. They appear to be arguing over who should be in charge of the rabbit which is being spit-roasted over an open fire. On seeing you, they cease their argument and draw their short swords. You are going to have to fight the ORCS advancing towards you.

|  | SKILL | STAMINA |
|---|---|---|
| First ORC | 5 | 5 |
| Second ORC | 5 | 6 |

If you win the battle, turn to **383**. If you wish to *Escape* during the battle, you may do so by running back to the path and heading north. Turn to **254**.

## 30

Lose 2 STAMINA points for the deep cut on your forehead. If you are still alive, turn to **225**.

## 31

You crawl out of the tunnel and step on to the ladder on the wall of the well. You climb out of the well and return to the path. Turn to **362**.

## 32

You reach into your backpack and hand over 10 Gold Pieces and two objects to Arragon. Make the necessary deductions to your Equipment List. Arragon then commands you to leave and you run out of the cottage back to the junction in the path. Lose 1

LUCK point and head north along the path. Turn to **150**.

## 33
The friar shakes his head, saying, 'There doesn't seem to be any charity in the world any more.' With a shrug of the shoulders he sets off south again. You watch him disappear before continuing your journey north. Turn to **390**.

## 34
As you rub the lantern, green smoke slowly starts to rise from the wick and take shape. It forms the outline of a fat old man with a bald head sitting on a cushion. His mouth opens slowly and in a deep voice he says, 'Well, what do you want?' You tell him of your quest but he tells you he is unable to offer you material gain or wealth. He can only offer you personal well-being. You may restore your SKILL, STAMINA or LUCK score to its *Initial* level. As soon as you make your choice, the genie disappears and the lantern turns black. You throw it to the ground and head north. Turn to **231**.

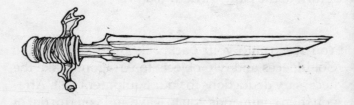

## 35

Lose 4 STAMINA points for the injury caused by the terrible burn. If you are still alive turn to **132**.

## 36

Thinking about the robed stranger you feel a little uncomfortable. There was something about his manner that you did not trust. You stop to take a look in your backpack and are annoyed to find something is missing. The man was a thief! Deduct either all your remaining Gold Pieces or two of the magic items you may have purchased from Yaztromo from your *Adventure Sheet*. You are in two minds whether or not to run after the thief but you sense that he will not be where he said he was going. You curse and start off north again. Turn to **187**.

## 37

You reach into the tree and pluck a pear-shaped fruit which is purple in colour. You take a small bite and it tastes very bitter. If you wish to spit it out and continue north up the path, turn to **226**. If you would rather swallow the fruit, turn to **336**.

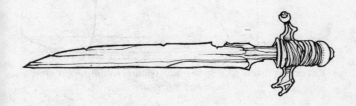

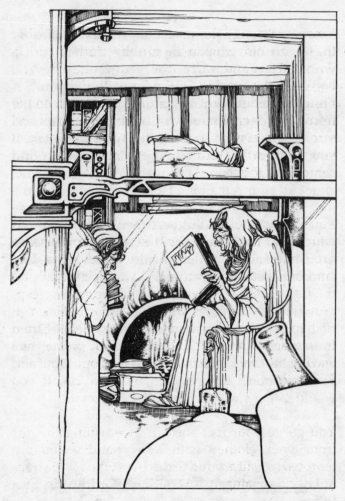

**38** *You can see an old woman in grubby clothes reading one of several books by the fireside.*

## 38

You peer through the small dirty window of the hut to see an old woman in grubby clothes with a wrinkled face and warty nose reading one of several books by the fireside on the far wall of the hut. A hunchbacked servant is carrying more books to her from shelves crammed with old books, charts and scrolls. If you want to enter the hut, turn to **315**. If you would rather return to the path and head north again, turn to **220**.

## 39

You spread the net out and then whirl it around your head. You release it in the direction of the Cave Troll and watch as it flies silently through the air to land on its stationary target. It wraps itself around the Cave Troll, who wakes quickly from his sleep, growls loudly and tries to struggle from the net. You rush to the stone chair and take the leather bag from the enraged Cave Troll. You run out of the cave leaving the Cave Troll to fight his way out of the net. Turn to **287**.

## 40

You get to your feet and curse, brushing the dirt from your clothes with your hands. You are tempted to wait around to discover who set the trap, but decide against it. To continue northwards, turn to **274**.

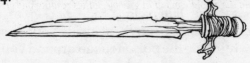

**41**

You run back down the path to the junction where the crow is still sitting on the signpost. You turn left, and run eastwards, shouting, 'Good afternoon!' to the crow as you pass him. Turn to **239**.

**42**

The old woman throws back her head and roars with laughter as you start to make conversation. She is an evil woman. Lose 1 LUCK point and draw your sword. Turn to **342**.

**43**

You draw your sword and charge the Wild Hill Men, who stop their argument and turn towards you, screaming and wielding axes.

|  | SKILL | STAMINA |
|---|---|---|
| First WILD HILL MAN | 7 | 5 |
| Second WILD HILL MAN | 6 | 4 |

Fight them one at a time. If you win, turn to **50**. You may *Escape* by running north along the path. Turn to **188**.

**44**

Lose 2 STAMINA points. If you are still alive, you find your Nose Filters in a side pocket of your backpack and hastily slip them inside your nostrils. You slowly inhale the poisonous air around you, but all is well and you are able to breathe freely. After a while the gas cloud fades away. However, there does not seem to be much point in staying here any longer and you walk over to the steps on the far wall. Turn to **293**.

### 45

Lose 2 STAMINA points. If you are still alive, turn to **165**.

### 46

The carrot flies through the air but before it reaches the Gnome it changes into a butterfly and flutters away on the breeze. The Gnome starts to whittle a piece of wood with a small knife and has a bored expression on his face. Lose 2 LUCK points. You decide that you ought to treat him with a little more respect and apologize to the Gnome. Turn to **12**.

### 47

While you are distracted by the servant the Witch shouts some strange words into the air. Suddenly she vanishes in a bright flash and reappears as a small bat which flies out of the open door. On seeing this, the hunchback slumps to the floor and starts to cry. You may:

| | |
|---|---|
| Search the hut for something useful | Turn to **26** |
| Leave the hut and return to the path to head north | Turn to **220** |

**49** *Standing in the middle of the cave are two green-skinned creatures with small bodies and large heads.*

## 48

You lift the chest above your head and send it crashing to the floor. It bursts open and amidst the splintered wood lies a large, light blue egg nearly a metre round. You tap it with your finger. It is cold and hard, and feels like marble. Suddenly a crack appears and before you can move the egg explodes, sending fragments of razor-sharp shell flying through the air. Roll one die to determine how many splinters of shell stick in you, and lose 1 STAMINA point for each. If you are still alive, you stagger out of the room and continue north along the path. Turn to **288**.

## 49

You press on down the tunnel into the cave entrance. The roof of the cave is no higher than the tunnel and you are unable to stand up. The cave is very small and filled with tiny bits of furniture and all manner of objects and curios. Standing in the middle of the cave are two green-skinned creatures with small bodies and large heads; they have pointed ears and long noses and their clothes are made from sacks. They appear very alarmed and charge at you with their daggers. You must fight the GREMLINS as you are unable to turn round and escape.

|                | SKILL | STAMINA |
|----------------|-------|---------|
| First GREMLIN  | 4     | 3       |
| Second GREMLIN | 3     | 2       |

You fight the Gremlins one at a time but must reduce your Attack Strength by 3 for each round of combat because you are fighting on your hands and knees. If you win, turn to **371**.

### 50

Around the neck of one of the Wild Hill Men you find a small silver key hanging on a small leather cord. You untie the leather cord and put the key in your backpack. You set off north again – turn to **188**.

### 51

Your walk along the green valley floor brings you to a junction in the path. If you want to head north, turn to **199**. If you wish to continue east, turn to **397**.

### 52

Quin explains that he will wager some Dust of Levitation against an item or coins to the value of 10 Gold Pieces. As you sit down at the table opposite him, you deftly slip the Armband of Strength on to your arm. You put your elbow on to the table and lock hands with him. His grip is like an iron jaw and his dark slanted eyes look confident. His biceps

bulge and he gives the signal for the contest to begin. You start to push his arm down and are amazed at your own strength. Sweat breaks out on his forehead and you can see the disbelief and pain on his face. You push harder and force his arm on to the table in defeat – turn to **78**.

### 53

The muscles in your neck start to stiffen and you feel the effects of the poison from the darts running through your body. You pluck the darts from your neck, but it's too late. You sink to your knees and then roll over unconscious. When you wake up, you find that you still have your sword and possessions, but all your gold is gone. The Pygmies have stolen it all. You shake your fist at the unseen thieves and start to walk north again along the path. Turn to **92**.

### 54

As you draw your sword, Yaztromo turns round and casually advises you not to be foolish as his magic is great. If you still wish to attack him, turn to **399**. If you change your mind and decide to follow him up the stairs, turn to **261**.

**57** *You hear a loud roar and look up to see a dragon-like creature flying down to its lair.*

## 55

You reach into your backpack and pull out the purple silk glove. It fits snugly on your hand. Then you bend down and pick up a good-sized rock and take aim. You throw the rock with all your might at the Ogre and it flies like an arrow to hit him on the side of the head, knocking him unconscious. The creature in the cage jumps around even more frantically than before. Do you:

| | |
|---|---|
| Take a closer look at the creature in the cage? | Turn to **168** |
| Search through the contents of the cave? | Turn to **313** |
| Leave the cave immediately and continue northwards? | Turn to **358** |

## 56

Walking along the tranquil valley floor, you arrive at a junction in the path. You see that the way south leads back to the hills so decide to dismiss that option. If you wish to continue west, turn to **233**. If you wish to head north, turn to **163**.

## 57

You walk over to investigate the lair but are suddenly aware of a dark shadow being cast all about you. You hear a loud roar above you and look up to see a dragon-like creature with two legs and green scaly skin flying down to its lair. A bolt of fire shoots from its mouth towards you. *Test your Luck*. If you are Lucky, the fire bolt misses you and explodes by your feet – turn to **132**. If you are Unlucky, the fire bolt slams into your back, knocking you to the ground – turn to **35**.

## 58

You reach into your backpack and pull out the small bottle of Holy Water. Quickly removing the cork you throw the water at the advancing GHOUL. Thick smoke rises into the air from the burn marks made by the Holy Water on the putrid flesh of the Ghoul. The Ghoul appears to be in great pain but through its wide-open mouth no sound is heard. It crawls into a corner of the room, desperate to escape your goodly weapon. You walk over to the coffin and look inside. You are overjoyed to see, as well as 25 Gold Pieces, an object that the Ghoul was using as a head rest – a bronze hammer head with the letter G inscribed in it. You happily put your findings into your backpack and walk back up the stairs to leave the crypt and return to the path to head north. Turn to **112**.

### 59

You arrive at another junction in the path. Ignoring the way south, you continue east – turn to **171**.

### 60

You hold your breath and reach into your backpack, frantically searching for your Nose Filters. *Test your Luck*. If you are Lucky, you find them straight away and slip them inside your nostrils – turn to **183**. If you are Unlucky, you are unable to find them quickly enough and are forced to inhale the poisonous gas – turn to **44**.

### 61

Soon you are back at the first junction. If you wish to crawl south back to the well, turn to **398**. If you wish to continue east, turn to **151**.

### 62

As you draw your sword from your last opponent the white stallion gallops off east along the path out of sight. You turn and set off west again. Turn to **208**.

## 63

On seeing the arrow fly past you the Centaur rears up on his hind legs and then charges into a gallop straight at you. You have to jump back to avoid being run down. He gallops past you in a cloud of dust and stops some ten metres away down the path you have just come along. Maybe fighting the noble Centaur is not such a good idea after all. You sheathe your sword and decide to wade across the river. Turn to **178**.

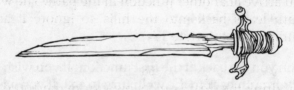

## 64

Before the Tangleweed can drag you to the ground you manage to grab the bottle containing the Potion of Plant Control from your backpack and gulp down its contents. As if touched by flame the Tangleweed releases your limbs and retreats from the path. You decide to run quickly along the path while the effects of the potion still last. Turn to **142**.

## 65

The bridge is in a terrible state of repair, but you manage to cross it safely. You are at the foot of some hills and it is getting darker as night closes in. You pitch camp behind some rocks to the left of the path and settle down to sleep with your sword by your side. Turn to **330**.

## 66

You step carefully along the slippery stones to the other side of the river. You see that the path continues north into the hills but as it is getting dark you decide to make camp for the night under a large solitary tree to the right of the path. You build a large fire and settle down to sleep with your sword by your side. Turn to **325**.

## 67

You arrive at another junction in the path. The way south leads back into the hills so ignore it and continue west (turn to **113**).

## 68

You drink the clear liquid slowly from the bottle. It tastes very bitter and you are apprehensive about what you have done. But then a glow radiates through your body and you feel invigorated. You have drunk a health potion – add 3 STAMINA points to your score. You set off east along the path. Turn to **59**.

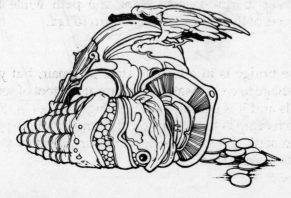

**69** *Small, pale-skinned humanoids appear to be tending crops of different-coloured fungi.*

## 69

The tunnel goes deeper underground, heading west some sixty metres before opening out into a vast cavern with green slimy walls. A shaft of daylight shines down from the roof of the cavern illuminating the floor. Small, pale-skinned humanoids are scattered about and they appear to be tending crops of different-coloured fungi. A stream trickles through the cavern. Stone steps rise past alcoves on the far wall to a hole in the roof through which the daylight streams. You draw your sword and approach one of the small humanoids. As you get nearer you see that they are hairless and their eyes are blank. They seem totally uninterested in your presence, walking slowly between their rows of fungi and bending down occasionally to remove unwelcome insects and weeds from the crops. You may:

| | |
|---|---|
| Attack one of the small humanoids | Turn to **264** |
| Chop down one of the fungi | Turn to **143** |
| Demand to eat a green-topped fungus | Turn to **269** |
| Demand to eat a red-topped fungus | Turn to **16** |

## 70

The sword is magnificent and was obviously made by a master craftsman. It feels powerful in your hand. Add 2 points to your current SKILL score for your enchanted sword. Cutting your new weapon through the air you set off north down the gorge (turn to **334**).

### 71

On pulling back the curtain you see a tiny green-skinned creature with a large head. He has a long nose and pointed ears and wears brown canvas clothing. A large medallion hangs from his neck on a silver chain. The creature is sitting at a table examining a red clay figure of a human hand. On seeing you enter the cave he takes a stone hammer and smashes the clay hand. He is a GREMLIN chief and jumps to his feet to face you with his hammer. You must fight him.

GREMLIN        SKILL 5       STAMINA 5

During each Attack Round you must reduce your Attack Strength by 3 because of your cramped fighting position. If you win, turn to **273**.

### 72

The path ends at a junction. The way south leads back to the forest so you decide to head north (turn to **138**).

### 73

You step back and then charge at the door. Roll two dice. If the number rolled is equal to or less than both your LUCK and SKILL scores, the door flies open – turn to **327**. If the number rolled is greater than either your LUCK or SKILL score, you bounce off the door and rub your bruised shoulder. You decide against risking any further injury to yourself and return to the path to head north (turn to **112**).

## 74

You lift the leather bag off the back of the stone chair and tiptoe out of the cave. Outside you stop to examine the contents of the bag. Inside you find 5 Gold Pieces and a small brass bell. You put these in your backpack and walk back to the junction in the path to head north. Turn to **25**.

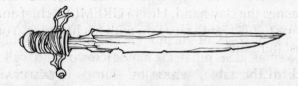

## 75

Your legs feel very vulnerable and you half expect them to be bitten any moment by some unseen river creature. However, nothing happens and you manage to cross safely. You are now at the foot of some hills and it is getting darker as night closes in. You decide to camp behind some rocks to the left of the path and settle down to sleep with your sword by your side. Turn to **330**.

## 76

The path turns suddenly to the right and proceeds northwards into the dense undergrowth. Turn to **206**.

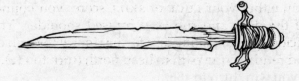

### 77

The Pygmies quickly turn and run off into the grasses. Will you:

Draw your sword and run into the
grass after them?      Turn to **377**
Continue north along the path?      Turn to **92**

### 78

Quin stands up and walks silently to a wooden chest at the back of the hut. He lifts the lid and pulls out a small glass phial. He hands it to you and walks back to the table, where he slumps in his chair looking thoroughly dejected. The dust in the phial sparkles in the light and you put it into your backpack and leave the hut. Outside you walk back to the junction in the path. Turn to **349**.

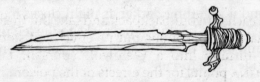

### 79

You stand with your back to the tree and prepare to fight the Vampire Bats. You fight them one at a time as they swoop down on you.

|  | SKILL | STAMINA |
|---|---|---|
| First VAMPIRE BAT | 5 | 5 |
| Second VAMPIRE BAT | 6 | 5 |
| Third VAMPIRE BAT | 5 | 7 |

If you win, turn to **386**.

## 80

There does not seem to be much point in staying here any longer and you walk over to the steps in the far wall. Turn to **293**.

## 81

Ahead you hear high-pitched voices frantically calling to each other. The tunnel ends at a small cave entrance. Suddenly an arrow flies out of the cave towards you. *Test your Luck*. If you are Lucky, the arrow whistles past your head (turn to **49**). If you are Unlucky, it lodges in your shoulder (turn to **4**).

## 82

Do you possess a Potion of Stillness? If you do, turn to **235**. If you do not, turn to **13**.

## 83

You reach for your backpack and take out the belladonna. It is poisonous but its effect will stop you from turning into a Werewolf yourself. Lose 2 STAMINA points for the effects of the poison. If you are still alive, turn to **139**.

## 84

As you approach the boulder you are even more surprised to see it suddenly rise up on what appear to be two stumpy stone legs. Then two stone arms with huge club-shaped fists spring out of its sides. You stare in disbelief as the boulder lumbers towards you and raises one of its great stone fists. You snap out of your bewilderment and draw your sword to fight the BOULDER BEAST.

BOULDER BEAST     SKILL 8     STAMINA 11

If you win, turn to **146**. You may *Escape* after three Attack Rounds by running north down the path into the valley. Turn to **245**.

## 85

Inside the cage a small, sinewy creature with brown, scaly skin is jumping up and down. He is a GOBLIN, and he has a black shiny rod hanging on a leather cord round his neck. If you want to unlock the cage door, turn to **9**. If you want to ignore the creature and leave the cave to continue your journey northwards, turn to **358**.

## 86

As you crouch down in the tall grass you hear the sound of galloping hooves amidst the barking. Then you see the legs of four hounds and one horse race past you in a cloud of dust. The sound of the hunt quickly fades into the distance and you step out on to the path again. Wondering about the poor old fox you set off west once more. Turn to **208**.

### 87

The path leads along a ridge of the hill and comes to another junction. You see that the way south leads back to the river, so you decide to head north again. Turn to **90**.

### 88

Climbing the steps you soon reach the second alcove. You see vague shapes in the dark and hear the sound of shuffling feet. If you wish to enter the alcove, turn to **212**. If you wish to continue climbing, turn to **107**.

### 89

The coin lands in the water with a gentle plop (make the deduction to your Equipment List). You wish for more Gold Pieces but nothing happens – this is not a wishing well. You may:

| | |
|---|---|
| Descend the ladder to look down the tunnel | Turn to **256** |
| Return to the path to head east | Turn to **281** |
| Return to the path to head west | Turn to **238** |

**90** *Two sinewy men with long hair and beards spring from behind a boulder.*

**90**

The path runs north down the hill between large boulders and rocks. You have an uneasy feeling that you are being watched. Then, from behind one of the larger boulders to the left of the path, spring two sinewy men with long hair and beards. They are wearing animal furs and look menacing. One notches an arrow to his bow and lets it fly. *Test your Luck.* If you are Lucky, the arrow misses you and flies past your head (turn to **210**). If you are Unlucky, the arrow lodges itself in your shoulder and you suffer the loss of 3 STAMINA points. If you are still alive, turn to **348**

**91**

You open the book and are surprised to see that the pages are hollowed out in the middle. Lying in the cavity is a small jewel on a silver chain. Beside it is a parchment which reads:

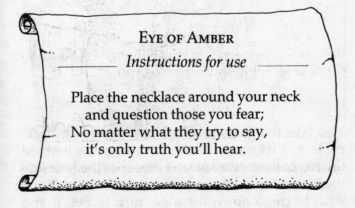

EYE OF AMBER

*Instructions for use*

Place the necklace around your neck
and question those you fear;
No matter what they try to say,
it's only truth you'll hear.

You place the necklace around your neck and presume your find will come in useful in this evil forest! Add 1 LUCK point. Leaving the hut you return to the path and head north – turn to **220**.

## 92

As the path proceeds northwards, the grass becomes shorter and the ground starts to rise gently. Ahead you can hear the sound of flowing water. However, much more ominous, you also hear another sound, above you in the sky – a loud buzzing noise. Suddenly a swarm of large bees, each bee some ten centimetres long, is hovering directly above you. You may:

| | |
|---|---|
| Try to run to the water ahead and dive in | Turn to **299** |
| Stand and fight | Turn to **7** |
| Drink a Potion of Insect Control (if you have one) | Turn to **100** |

## 93

Back at the junction you may either go east (turn to **61**) or keep going south (turn to **270**).

## 94

You take the Rope of Climbing out of your backpack. As if it knows what to do, it wraps itself round the top of the tree trunk and descends the hole into the tunnel below, inviting you to climb down. If you wish to climb down the rope, turn to **136**. If you wish to change your mind and return to the path to head north again, turn to **144**.

## 95

You try with all your might to move the stone slab, but it will not budge. Do you have any Dust of Levitation? If you do, turn to **173**. If not, turn to **368**.

## 96

As you lift your arm to strike the dog it growls fiercely and leaps at you.

HUNTING DOG  SKILL 7  STAMINA 6

If you defeat the Hunting Dog, you must now fight the other three dogs and their master in pairs. Both members of a pair will have a separate attack on you in each Attack Round, but you must choose which of the two you will fight. Attack your nominated target as in a normal battle. Against the other you will throw for your Attack Strength in the normal way, but you will not wound it if your Attack Strength is greater – you must count this as though you have just parried its blow. Of course if its Attack Strength is greater, it will have wounded you in the normal way.

|  |  | SKILL | STAMINA |
|---|---|---|---|
| First pair: | HUNTING DOG | 6 | 6 |
|  | HUNTING DOG | 5 | 6 |
| Second pair: | HUNTING DOG | 6 | 5 |
|  | MASKED MAN | 8 | 7 |

If you win, turn to **62**.

**99** *You see a large man with dark skin sitting at a table in the middle of the hut.*

## 97

The path leads ever northwards but at last the trees are beginning to thin out and appear less menacing as daylight streams through between them. On the right-hand side of the path you see an old oak chair covered with moss. If you wish to sit in the chair to rest and eat, turn to **328**. If you would rather press on northwards, turn to **118**.

## 98

On your long walk around Darkwood Forest you are attacked by a large group of Wild Hill Men, probably the same group who attacked Bigleg and his party two days earlier. *Test your Luck*. If you are Lucky, you manage to run away from them without being hit by the rain of arrows which falls all about you; turn to **1**. If you are Unlucky, you slip and fall as you run, pierced by many arrows. Your adventure ends here.

## 99

Ahead you see that the path ends at the door of a large hut made of dried mud. It has a domed roof and a single window. You peer through the window and see a large man with dark skin sitting at a table in the middle of the hut. He is bare-chested and is flexing the muscles of his arms. If you wish to enter the hut, turn to **209**. If you would rather return to the junction in the path, turn to **349**.

**100**

As you reach into your backpack, you realize with horror that the large, buzzing insects above you are KILLER BEES. You grab the bottle marked Potion of Insect Control and gulp down its contents. The Killer Bees dive down to attack you, but are suddenly repelled as though they have hit an invisible screen. They hover all around you buzzing loudly but do not sting you. With new heart you draw your sword and swing it through the air. You catch one of the Killer Bees and it falls to the ground. You step on it with your leather sandal. The others then fly off into the distance. You continue northwards towards the sound of flowing water. Turn to **339**.

**101**

You lift the leather bag off the stone chair and walk outside. Examining the contents of the bag you find 5 Gold Pieces and a small brass bell. You put these in your backpack and walk back to the junction in the path to head north. Turn to **25**.

**102**

Walking along the path you notice marks in the ground made by the hooves of a horse heading east. You soon arrive at another junction in the path. The hoof marks lead south, back to the forest. You decide to head north. Turn to **105**.

**103**

The path opens out into a small clearing. To your right you see a pile of branches, grass and pieces of rag, the lair of some large creature. Amongst the debris and old bones scattered about you catch sight of something glittering. If you want to look more closely, turn to **57**. If you wish to hurry north along the path, turn to **360**.

The BANDIT woman steps forward with her sword raised, shouting 'Death to the intruder!' She is their leader and you must fight her first.

BANDIT        SKILL 8        STAMINA 6

If you manage to defeat her, you must now fight the other four Bandits in pairs. Both members of a pair will have a separate attack on you in each Attack Round, but you must choose which of the two you will fight. Attack your chosen Bandit as in a normal battle. Against the other you will throw for your Attack Strength in the normal way, but you will not wound it if your Attack Strength is greater; you must count this as though you have just fended off his blow. Of course if his Attack Strength is greater, he will have wounded you in the normal way.

|  |  | SKILL | STAMINA |
|---|---|---|---|
| First pair: | BANDIT A | 7 | 6 |
|  | BANDIT B | 6 | 4 |
| Second pair: | BANDIT A | 7 | 5 |
|  | BANDIT B | 5 | 6 |

If you win, turn to **311**.

**107** *A huge dark shape steps out from the alcove with flame shooting from its nostrils.*

### 105

In the distance to the right of the path you see large birds circling in the sky. As you get closer you recognize them as vultures. If you wish to step off the path to see what or whom the vultures are interested in, turn to **384**. If you wish to ignore the vultures and continue walking north, turn to **394**.

### 106

There is a fire-blackened copper kettle in the ashes of the fire which you pick up to inspect. You remove the lid and find a gold ring with a large emerald set in it. It has a value of 15 Gold Pieces. You are very fortunate and may add 2 LUCK points. Happy with your new treasure you decide to ignore the wooden chest and leave the room to continue northwards. Turn to **288**.

### 107

Just as you reach the last steps before the next alcove, a jet of flame shoots out to bar your way. Then a huge dark shape steps out from the alcove with flame shooting from its nostrils. Black smoke curls up into the air. The beast is shaped like a man, but has wings and carries a flaming sword in one hand and a whip in the other. A golden crown sits on its head. It faces you motionless on the steps above you. Suddenly it cracks its whip and raises its fiery sword. The only way out of this cavern lies before you at the top of the steps. To get there, you will have to fight the FIRE DEMON, master of the clones:

FIRE DEMON       SKILL 10       STAMINA 10

In addition to its normal attack with its fiery sword, throw one die every Attack Round for its whip. On a roll of 1 or 2, the whip will lash you and 1 point must be subtracted from your STAMINA. A roll of 3 to 6 means the whip misses you. It is possible to use your LUCK against the whip. If you win turn to **152**.

**108**

The pain increases and becomes almost unbearable. You grip your stomach with your arms and fall to your knees, foaming at the mouth. Eventually the pain subsides but you are very weak after your ordeal. Lose 3 STAMINA points. You ponder what else might be in store for you in this forest and decide to turn north up the path. Turn to **226**.

**109**

Soon the path leads out of the trees on to a large plain with tall grasses. Beyond it you see rising ground and, further off, some low hills. The path splits and goes in three directions.

| | |
|---|---|
| If you want to go west | Turn to **124** |
| If you want to go east | Turn to **72** |
| If you want to continue north | Turn to **309** |

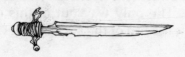

## 110

If you wish to search through the Gremlin's leather backpack, turn to **257**. If you wish to leave the tunnel without any further delay, turn to **31**.

## 111

The expression on Arragon's face changes from confidence to fear. Perhaps he is not all that he makes himself out to be. Suddenly he apologizes for being so aggressive but explains that these lands are filled with bandits and murderers and he has to protect himself by pretending to be a wizard of supreme power. He begs forgiveness and offers you 5 Gold Pieces if you will leave him in peace and tell nobody of his disguise. You accept his offer and leave the cottage. You walk back to the junction in the path and head north; turn to **150**.

## 112

The path presses on northwards through the dense trees. Then it makes a sudden turn to the right and heads east. The path is so overgrown in places that you have to use your sword to cut through it. Your walk east is long and tiring. At last you reach a junction in the path. Looking at Bigleg's map you decide to head north again in the direction of Stonebridge and ignore the narrow path continuing east. Turn to **103**.

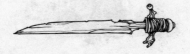

### 113

The path makes a sudden turn to the right and heads north across the valley floor. To the left of the path you see a large pond with a small wooden hut with a thatched roof by its edge. If you want to investigate the hut, turn to **324**. If you wish to ignore the hut and continue north along the path, turn to **149**.

### 114

The Treeman lumbers slowly towards you on large, splayed roots. If you possess Fire Capsules, turn to **350**. If you do not possess them, draw your sword and turn to **123**.

### 115

The path soon comes to a junction. If you wish to go west, turn to **382**. If you wish to go east, turn to **277**.

## 116

Eventually you manage to get back to sleep but are awake early. In the morning light you notice a gold-studded leather collar round the neck of the largest Wolf. It must be worth 15 Gold Pieces. Putting the collar in your backpack you wonder who the Wolf's owner might be. You collect your belongings and head north along the path. Turn to **314**.

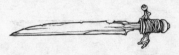

## 117

You unlock the door and step back, drawing your sword in case the Goblin tries to attack you. He picks up a wooden stool and, waving it in the air, kicks the door open and charges at you screaming. You must fight.

GOBLIN          SKILL 5          STAMINA 4

If you win, turn to **232**.

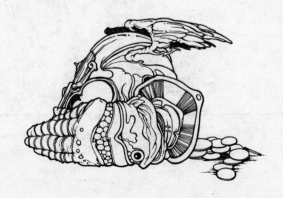

**118** *A large brown pig-like creature bursts out on to the path and halts there.*

## 118

The path eventually emerges from the trees on to a vast plain. Beyond you see rising ground leading to low hills. The waist-high grasses on either side of the path sway gently in the warm breeze. All is peaceful and the dangers ahead seem unimportant. You are enjoying your walk when suddenly the silence is broken by the sound of squealing and grunting to the right of the path. You can see a path being made through the grass by an unseen beast moving quickly towards you. You draw your sword in readiness. A few yards ahead of you a large brown pig-like creature bursts out on to the path and halts there. It has two long tusks protruding from a short stubby snout. Steam rises into the air from its sweating body. Its small eyes look at you before it puts its head down to charge at you. You must fight the WILD BOAR.

WILD BOAR        SKILL 6        STAMINA 5

If you win, turn to **174**.

## 119

The ground is quite steep as the path wends its way into the hills. By the time you reach the top the sun is quite hot. All around in the distance you see the green circle of Darkwood Forest. Mist still hangs in the tall grass behind you, but ahead you see a valley floor bathed in sunlight. All is quiet. As you start down the far side of the hill you see a junction in the path. You may either continue north down the hill (turn to **90**) or head west along the new branch (turn to **216**).

**120**

You drop a stone down the hollow tree trunk to the tunnel below. It must be some five metres to the bottom. Do you possess a Rope of Climbing? If you do, turn to **94**. If you do not, turn to **380**.

**121**

Back at the junction you may either go east (turn to **61**) or keep going north (turn to **81**).

**122**

At the bottom of the ladder you see that the tunnel runs quite a distance north. You are surprised to see that it is lit by torches at regular intervals along its length. If you wish to crawl along the tunnel, turn to **135**. If you wish to climb back up the ladder and return to the path, turn to **362**.

**123**

The Treeman lashes out at you with two of its main branches and you leap into the attack.

TREEMAN      SKILL 8      STAMINA 8

You must defeat the Treeman twice, once for each main branch, before it will die. If you win, turn to **27**. You may *Escape* during battle by running back to the junction in the path – turn to **234**.

## 124

The path ends at another junction. The way south leads back to the forest so you decide to head north. Turn to **180**.

## 125

As you descend into the hole, you notice large amounts of slime secreted by some huge creature. If you wish to climb back out of the hole and continue walking northwards up the path, turn to **337**. If you wish to carry on down the hole, turn to **15**.

## 126

You gently prise the lid off the box, but as you do so, a yellow gas escapes and envelops your face. If you possess Nose Filters, turn to **365**. If not, turn to **22**.

## 127

You climb on to the Centaur's back and he turns and walks into the river. The water is a dark green colour and you wonder what kind of creatures might be lurking in its depths. Soon you reach the other side and you pay the Centaur his 3 Gold Pieces. He thanks you and waves goodbye, wishing you good luck. You are now at the foot of some hills and it is beginning to get dark. You see the path winding its way north up into the hills. You decide to camp under a great, old oak tree to the right of the path and settle down to sleep with your sword by your side. Turn to **298**.

**130** *A creature which appears to be half-cat and half-girl is lying on a branch over the path.*

## 128

You cut the thick ropes holding the Barbarian. He grunts, and sits up to rub his wrists and ankles. He looks at you and sneers. He is either delirious or ungrateful, for he pulls out one of the wooden stakes from the ground and turns to attack you!

BARBARIAN          SKILL 9          STAMINA 7

If you win, turn to **272**.

## 129

Your arm is sore from the effort and the loss of gold to Quin makes you dejected. Lose 2 LUCK points. You leave the hut and the smiling Quin. Outside you walk back to the junction in the path. Turn to **349**.

## 130

The path forces its way through the gnarled trees and thorny bushes. You hear growling above you and look up to see a creature which appears to be half-cat and half-girl lying on a branch over the path. It has short black shiny fur like a panther but there are paws at the end of its arms and legs with sharp claws. Its face has human features with slanted eyes and long teeth. It looks as if it is about to pounce. If you wish to draw your sword and fight the CATWOMAN, turn to **153**. If you wish to run quickly ahead, lose 1 LUCK point and turn to **355**.

## 131

You drag yourself out of the water on the far bank of the river. You see that the path continues north into the hills but as it is getting dark, you decide to make camp for the night under a large solitary tree to the right of the path. You build a large fire and settle down to sleep with your sword by your side. Turn to **325**.

## 132

The creature landing in front of you is a WYVERN. It looks at you and opens its huge mouth to let out another burning roar. It is about ten metres long and its thick scales look hard to penetrate with your sword. Do you possess a flute? If you do, turn to **258**. If you do not, turn to **167**.

## 133

Slipping the ring on to your middle finger you are suddenly gripped by an agonizing pain. Eventually the pain subsides but you are unable to take off the ring. You are wearing a cursed Ring of Slowness which will force you to subtract 2 points from all future dice rolls when computing your own Attack

Strength during combat. Note this on your Equipment List. If you wish to try on the gauntlet, turn to **374**. If wish to ignore the gauntlet (or have already tried it on) you must walk north again along the path – turn to **360**.

### 134

You make a wish but nothing happens. Lose 1 LUCK point. If you wish to rub some hot mud on to your wounds, turn to **283**. If you wish to set off north along the path, turn to **303**.

### 135

The tunnel continues north until at last you arrive at a junction. If you wish to crawl west, turn to **284**. If you wish to crawl east, turn to **151**.

### 136

You climb down the rope to the tunnel below. Soon your eyes become accustomed to the dark and you see that the tunnel is only one metre high. You must crawl along on your hands and knees to explore it. Turn to **69**.

### 137

If you possess a Glove of Missile Dexterity, turn to **55**. If you do not, turn to **10**.

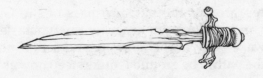

## 138

As you walk along the path through the waist-high grasses you watch the grass rippling in the wind. Soon you get the uncomfortable feeling that the grass has a will of its own and is moving independently of the wind. Suddenly a clump of grass stretches out across the path and wraps itself around your ankle. Other clumps of grass try to grab your arms and legs. You realize that you are surrounded by TANGLEWEED. If you have a Potion of Plant Control, turn to **64**. If you do not, turn to **159**.

## 139

The effects of the belladonna and the bite of the Werewolf wear off and you finally manage to get back to sleep. In the morning you collect your belongings and head north along the path into the hills. Turn to **198**.

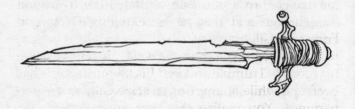

## 140

You step around the bulbous mass of the Giant Spider and settle down again to a nervous sleep. You awake early in the morning and set off north along the path. The ground is quite steep now as the path wends its way up into the hills. By the time you reach the top the sun is quite hot. All around in the distance you see the tight green circle of Darkwood Forest. Mist still hangs in the tall grasses behind you but ahead you see a valley floor bathed in sunlight. All is quiet. As you start down the far side of the hill, you see a junction in the path. You may:

Continue north down the hill       Turn to **25**
Go east along the new path       Turn to **267**

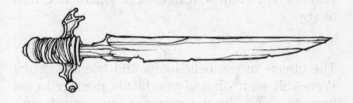

**141**

You ask the Dwarf if he comes from Stonebridge. He glares at you and jumps to his feet, grabbing his axe. He tells you that he hates the dwarfs of Stonebridge and that he is searching Darkwood Forest for Gillibran's war-hammer to take it back to his village, Mirewater, in the west. He tells you that his name is Trumble and that his favourite eagle has been lost while attempting to seize Gillibran's war-hammer. You realize that you are talking to an enemy of Stonebridge; lose 1 LUCK point. If you wish to attack Trumble, turn to **347**. If you wish to tell him that you are unable to help him, bid him farewell and continue east along the path – turn to **59**.

**142** *Standing proudly in front of you is a magnificent white beast, half-man, half-horse.*

## 142

As the path proceeds northwards, the grass becomes shorter and the ground starts to rise gently. Ahead you can hear the sound of flowing water. You soon reach the bank of a gently flowing river. There is no bridge but you see that the path continues north on the other side of the river. Standing proudly in front of you is a magnificent white beast, half-man, half-horse. A bow and a quiver of arrows are slung behind his back. He is a CENTAUR. Will you:

| | |
|---|---|
| Try to start a conversation with him? | Turn to 366 |
| Walk around him and wade into the river? | Turn to 178 |
| Draw your sword and attack him? | Turn to 251 |

## 143

Your sword cuts through the metre-high fungus as easily as if it were butter. A great cloud of spores is released from the stem making it difficult to breathe. You start to cough and splutter. Lose 2 STAMINA points. If you are still alive, turn to 80.

## 144

Continuing your walk along the valley floor you see the dark wall of Darkwood Forest looming up before you once again. The path leads directly into the thick undergrowth and soon you are walking between tall trees and crowded thorn bushes. It is dark and quiet. Before long, the path comes to a junction. If you wish to head west, turn to **213**. If you wish to head east, turn to **387**.

## 145

You untie the boat and start to row across the river to the far bank. You are about half-way when you notice that the bottom of the boat is beginning to fill with water. Leaks appear everywhere. The boat is rotten and starts to sink. You grab your possessions and swim across to the other side. You climb out of the river and are dismayed to see that all the remaining Provisions in your backpack (if you have any) have dissolved in the water. It is getting dark as night closes in and you decide to camp behind some rocks to the right of the path. You build a large fire and settle down to sleep with your sword by your side. Turn to **285**.

## 146

You look at the broken rock pile around your feet and wonder how such a beast ever came into being – perhaps from the misused power of an evil elementalist? You will never know. If you wish to take a piece of stone that was part of the Boulder Beast for later examination, note it on your Equipment List. You now return to the path and head north down into the valley. Turn to **245**.

## 147

The path heads north into the thick forest. In one of the few clearings between the trees you see smoke rising from the chimney of a wooden hut to your right. If you want to look through the window of the hut, turn to **38**. If you wish to keep walking north, turn to **220**.

## 148

The path continues north and you soon reach another junction. If you wish to continue north, turn to **97**. If you wish to go east, turn to **20**.

## 149

As you walk across the valley you see the dark green wall of Darkwood Forest looming up before you. The path leads directly into thick undergrowth and soon you are walking between tall dark trees and thorny bushes. It is dark and quiet. The path forks. If you wish to walk east, turn to **130**. If you would rather continue north, turn to **306**.

## 150

Walking north across the green valley you see the dark green wall of Darkwood Forest looming up before you. The path leads straight into the thick undergrowth and soon you are walking between tall dark trees and thorny bushes. It is dark and quiet and the path abruptly ends at a junction. If you wish to walk west, turn to **357**. If you wish to head east, turn to **171**.

## 151

The tunnel ends at a cave entrance. A curtain hangs over the entrance and you are unable to see inside. If you wish to throw back the curtain and enter the cave, turn to **71**. If you wish to turn round and return to the junction in the tunnel, turn to **296**.

## 152

In its dying throes the black Fire Demon is engulfed by its own fire. You step forward and grab its crown as it slumps to the ground in a smouldering heap. Its alcove lair is cold and dank. Inside there is a magnificent throne in front of which cower two Clone Warriors on their hands and knees, bowing to you in worship. You have defeated their master. You may:

| | |
|---|---|
| Place the crown on your head | Turn to **333** |
| Sit on the throne | Turn to **5** |
| Step over the Fire Demon and climb up to the roof | Turn to **249** |

## 153

The Catwoman growls and snarls before leaping down from the tree to attack you. You step back and prepare to fight.

CATWOMAN          SKILL 8          STAMINA 5

If you win, turn to **202**. You may *Escape* by running east along the path – turn to **355**.

## 154

You get to your feet and see that the Lantern has turned a dull black colour. You decide to have no more to do with it and set off north along the path (turn to **231**).

## 155

You settle down to sleep again but start to shake and tremble. Sweat pours from your body although you feel very cold. Do you possess any belladonna? If you do, turn to **83**. Otherwise turn to **259**.

## 156

Falling to the ground is becoming a bit of a bad habit! It is also beginning to hurt. Lose 3 STAMINA points for your injuries. If you are still alive, you get up and continue northwards along the path. Turn to **109**.

## 157

To the left of the path you notice a large hole in the ground with a diameter of some three metres. Walking over to the edge of the hole you see it sloping off into the depths of the earth. If you wish to walk down into the hole, turn to **125**. If you prefer to continue walking northwards up the path, turn to **337**.

## 158

You start to lose your balance as the illusion distorts your mind. You close your eyes and reach into your backpack, pulling out the Headband of Concentration, which you quickly place on your head. The spinning sensation in your head subsides and you open your eyes again to see the old woman who you now realize is a WITCH. To stop you reaching her, the servant throws a wooden chair at you. *Test your Luck.* If you are Lucky, the chair misses – turn to **47**. If you are Unlucky, the chair hits you on the side of the head, knocking you unconscious – turn to **353**.

**160** *You arrive at a moss-covered wooden signpost, on top of which sits a large crow.*

## 159

Despite your struggles the Tangleweed manages to grab your limbs and drag you to the ground. You see the grass begin to curl itself round your neck and tighten its grip. You choke and try to cough. But then you realize that the Tangleweed is not trying to strangle you – it is just trying to make as much contact as it can with your exposed flesh so that it can suck your blood! With horror, you see hundreds of tiny blood-ringed punctures on your arms and legs. Finally the weed, having drunk enough, releases its grip. Lose 3 STAMINA points. If you are still alive, you rise to your feet and stand shakily rubbing your wounds. Relieved to be alive, you start walking north again. Turn to **142**.

## 160

The narrow path continues to cut its way through the tangled forest. Strange animal cries and noises echo through the trees. At last the path widens to approximately a metre across. Soon you arrive at a moss-covered wooden signpost, on top of which sits a large crow. The arms of the signpost read 'North' and 'East'. Just as you are deciding which way to continue, you hear the words 'Good afternoon.' You look up in the direction of the voice and see the crow looking down at you inquisitively. 'Good afternoon . . .,' you reply slowly, feeling a little foolish. The crow speaks again, asking which way you are headed. You reply that you are looking for two goblins, small, sinewy creatures with brown, scaly skin. '1 Gold Piece will buy my advice,' states the crow confidently. Will you:

| | |
|---|---|
| Pay the crow for its advice? | Turn to **343** |
| Ignore the crow and turn north? | Turn to **8** |
| Ignore the crow and carry on eastwards? | Turn to **239** |

### 161

As your hand descends into the inky blackness of the vase it is gripped by an intense pain. First it feels as if it is being crushed and then it feels as if it is on fire. If you wish to pull your hand out of the vase, turn to **185**. If you want to feel around to find out what is inside the vase, turn to **341**.

### 162

There is nothing of use or value in the Fish Man's cave, so you walk round to the north side wall. Steps lead back through the waterfall and up the north wall of the gorge to the top. You are at the foot of some hills and can see the path climbing up into their midst in the north. It is getting dark and night

is closing in, so you decide to camp behind some rocks to the right of the path. You build a large fire and settle down to sleep with your sword by your side. Turn to **285**.

## 163

Although it is a bright sunny day a tiny grey cloud appears in the sky. It is very low and appears to be moving towards you. As it approaches you see that it is moving very quickly. Finally it hovers above you some five metres off the ground. Suddenly a bolt of lightning shoots out from the cloud, hitting you on the shoulder. Lose 3 STAMINA points. If you are still alive you see the cloud shoot off to the west at high speed. You pull yourself together and set off north again; turn to **375**.

## 164

You climb the last few steps and then you are out of the cavern standing on the rich green grass of the valley floor. To the east you see the hollow tree trunk down which you descended some time before. You pass it and return to the path, where you head north again. Turn to **144**.

## 165

The small Gremlin is agile, being able to run around you while you have difficulty in moving about on your hands and knees. You back up against a wall and draw your sword.

GREMLIN          SKILL 5          STAMINA 3

During each Attack Round you must reduce your Attack Strength by 3 because of your cramped fighting position. If you win, turn to 242.

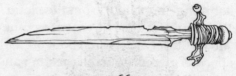

## 166

The friar smiles and says 'Bless you.' He bows and sets off south along the path, whistling as he goes. Add 2 LUCK points and head north (turn to 390).

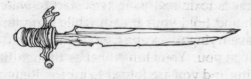

## 167

The Wyvern's long tail swishes from side to side and smoke curls up from its nostrils. You draw your sword and prepare to fight this fearsome monster.

WYVERN          SKILL 10          STAMINA 11

If you win, turn to 305.

**168**

Inside the cage a small, sinewy creature with brown, scaly skin is jumping up and down – he is a GOBLIN. Round his neck hangs a black shiny rod on a leather cord. If you want to unlock the cage door, turn to **117**. If you want to leave the cave and continue northwards, turn to **358**.

**169**

The gas is toxic and your eyes start to water. You cough and hold your breath while running round the cave trying to escape from the gas cloud which envelops you. Your lungs feel as though they are bursting and you are forced to inhale. Reduce your SKILL by 2 and your STAMINA by the amount of one die roll. If you are still alive you will see the gas cloud fade away. You put the silver box in your backpack. If you want to walk over to the creature in the cage, turn to **85**. If you would rather leave the cave to continue your journey northwards, turn to **358**.

**170** *Sitting at a desk is an old man wearing purple robes and a conical hat.*

### 170

You walk into a well-furnished room adorned with fine objects and woollen rugs. Sitting at a desk by the far wall of the room is an old man wearing purple robes and a conical hat. He rises from his chair and says, 'I am Arragon and you are an insignificant mortal. You have the nerve to walk into my household uninvited, no doubt to rob me of my wealth and treasure. You are wrong, stranger, for I will relieve you of your wealth. Unless you give me 10 Gold Pieces and two objects from your backpack to add to my exquisite collection, I will turn you to stone.' Are you wearing the Eye of Amber? If you are, turn to **223**. If not, turn to **346**.

### 171

The path comes to another junction. The way south leads back to the valley so you decide to stay in the forest and head north. Turn to **190**.

### 172

A ladder runs down the inside of the well to the water below. However, there appears to be a tunnel just above the surface of the water, running north. It is circular and has a diameter of one metre. You may:

| | |
|---|---|
| Toss a Gold Piece into the well to make a wish | Turn to **89** |
| Descend the ladder to look down the tunnel | Turn to **256** |
| Return to the path to head east | Turn to **281** |

### 173

You take from your backpack the glass phial containing the sparkling dust and sprinkle it on the stone slab. Slowly the stone slab starts to rise into the air. You peer into the box and are horrified to see a rotting corpse lying there. Ragged clothes cover a skeletal body with loose flesh hanging from it. You have lifted the lid off a coffin containing some cursed undead creature and jump back in horror as you see its eyes flick open. You are in a crypt made foul by some unknown follower of darkness. Slowly the creature rises out of its coffin and moves towards you with outstretched arms. Do you possess any Holy Water? If you do, turn to **58**. If not, turn to **227**.

### 174

As you draw your sword from the carcass of the Wild Boar you wonder what made it attack you. In the distance you hear the sound of barking dogs. Perhaps it was being hunted and, being trapped, made its last stand against you. Through the nose of the Boar you see a large gold ring which you cut loose and place in your backpack. It is worth 10 Gold Pieces. Add 1 LUCK point and turn to **323**.

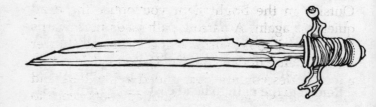

## 175

The iron lock on the chest is old and rusted and will not open. If you wish to try to lift the chest and smash it on the floor, turn to **372**. If you would rather leave it and rummage through the fireplace instead, turn to **106**.

## 176

You bend down over the lifeless body of the mad Goblin and examine the rod around its neck. The rod is made of ebony and there is a screw thread at one end. You are excited to see the letter G neatly inscribed at the other end of what must be the handle of the dwarfish war-hammer. You put your find in your backpack and leave the cave to continue your quest northwards. Turn to **358**.

## 177

Outside in the bright light you notice the dead quietness again. A narrow path leads northwards from the tall grass surrounding Yaztromo's tower into the dense undergrowth of Darkwood Forest. In a few strides you are surrounded by the dark and tangled forest; stones and knotted roots seem to

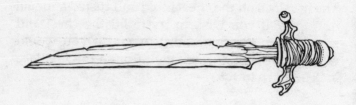

hide in the shadows and you can almost believe that
they are trying to trip you up. The light fades
quickly and the air becomes moist and unpleasant.
Deeper and deeper you go, into the gloom. Eventually the path forks on either side of a huge old tree.

To go west                          Turn to **289**
To go east                          Turn to **160**

**178**

As you wade into the river the Centaur gallops off
south down the path. The water is dark green in
colour and you wonder if any creatures lurk in its
depths. Although the water only rises to your waist
it is very cold and your legs feel numb. You think
something is touching your legs, maybe weeds, but
it is difficult to tell. Eventually you reach the far
bank and haul yourself out of the river. You look
down at your legs and are horrified to see a bloated
black Leech, some six inches long, clinging to your
thigh. You reach into your backpack and take salt
from your Provisions to rub on to the hideous
Leech. It curls up and falls off your leg. Lose one
portion of your Provisions. You kick the shrivelled

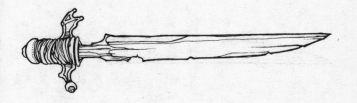

Leech back into the river and look around you. You are now at the foot of some hills and it is beginning to get dark. You see that the path winds its way north up into the hills and you decide to camp under a huge, old oak tree to the right of the path. Later you settle down to sleep with your sword by your side. Turn to **298**.

## 179

You place the helmet on your head. A surge of power starts to run through your body, making you feel strong and unafraid. The helmet has magical properties and will allow you to add 1 point to all future dice rolls when computing your own Attack Strength during combat so long as you wear it. Note this on your Equipment List. You start walking north again, pleased with your new armour. Turn to **115**.

## 180

Walking quickly along the path through waist-high grass, you arrive at another junction in the path. If you want to continue walking north, turn to **105**. If you wish to go west, turn to **361**.

**181** *A strange creature climbs out of the pool.*

## 181

You walk along the steps through the waterfall into a large cavern where there is a pool of still water. The steps run round the side of the pool and there is a stone table and chair on the far side. You go to the table and see fish scraps lying on it. Suddenly you hear a noise of splashing behind you. A strange creature climbs out of the pool and advances towards you armed with a trident. His legs are like a man's, but his face and torso resemble a large green fish with bulbous eyes. His arms are like yours but are covered with large scales. He is a FISH MAN and you must fight him.

FISH MAN            SKILL 7            STAMINA 6

If you win, turn to 162.

## 182

You take hold of the sword and place your foot against the rock. Roll two dice. If the number rolled is equal to or less than your current SKILL score, the sword slowly slides out of the rock (turn to 70). If the number rolled is greater than your current SKILL score, the sword will not move. You tire and are forced to give up and continue north down the gorge; turn to 334.

## 183

You slowly inhale the poisonous air around you, but all is well and you can breathe freely. After a while the gas cloud fades away. However, there does not seem to be much sense in staying here any longer and you walk over to the steps on the far wall. Turn to **293**.

### 184

You explain to the friar that you took a brass bell from a Cave Troll in the hills. You show it to him and he jumps for joy, shouting, 'Oh mercy, what fortune, what fortune.' He reaches into a leather pouch on the string belt around his waist and pulls out a small glass phial. You give him the brass bell and take the glass phial. You uncork the phial and drink its contents. Add 4 points to your STAMINA score. The friar shakes your hand, thanking you over and over again. At last you part company, with you continuing north and the friar walking south. Turn to **390**.

### 185

You are surprised to see no mark or sign of injury on your hand. You try to put your hand back into the vase but an invisible barrier across the opening stops you from doing so. You may either drop the vase to the ground to smash it (turn to **250**) or put it down on the porch and return to the path to head north again. Turn to **149**.

### 186

You step into the water and start to wade across the river. The water is quite murky and although the level only rises to your waist you feel somewhat vulnerable to the creatures that may live in the river. Suddenly your fears are realized – you feel sharp teeth sinking into your thigh. You reach down into the water and feel the long thin body of a BLOOD EEL extending from your leg. You draw your sword and start to stab at the water.

BLOOD EEL          SKILL 5          STAMINA 4

If you win, turn to **131**.

**187**

Walking along the twisting path you see a small, sinewy creature with brown, scaly skin sitting on a log on the right of the path. He has a sullen expression on his face as he slowly tosses a black shiny rod on a leather cord back and forth between his hands. He might be one of the Goblins you are looking for. Will you:

Draw your sword and attack
the Goblin?                          Turn to **286**
Try to start a conversation
with the Goblin?                     Turn to **203**
Ignore him and continue
walking north?                       Turn to **6**

**188**

Walking down the hill you see the valley floor stretching out ahead and, beyond, a sinister wall of trees – Darkwood! On the other side of the trees lies Stonebridge, your journey's end. Arriving on the valley floor you see that the path comes to a junction. If you want to head west, turn to **221**. If you want to head east, turn to **359**.

## 189

The green-topped fungi are being watered by two of the humanoids. If you want to eat some of the fungus, turn to **269**. If you wish to leave the cavern by the steps on the far wall, turn to **293**.

## 190

Ahead you hear the thumping of heavy footsteps and the noise of branches breaking. It sounds as though some huge creature is coming down the path towards you! If you wish to face the oncoming beast, turn to **265**. If you would rather hide in the bushes off the path, turn to **318**.

## 191

The friar is very nervous and jittery and shuffles from side to side as you start to speak. You ask him why he is so distraught and he tells you that his sacred brass bell has been stolen. As payment for its return he is willing to offer a magic healing potion. Do you have a brass bell? If you do, turn to **184**. If you do not, turn to **243**.

## 192

You draw your sword but the Gnome sits with his legs crossed and smiles. You look down at your hand and see that you are not holding your sword any longer – it has turned into a carrot! If you wish to apologize to the Gnome for being so rash, turn to **12**. If you would rather throw your carrot at him, turn to **46**.

## 193

A small green-skinned GREMLIN steps off the ladder to enter the tunnel. He stands no more than a metre high and is surprised to see you crouched in the tunnel. He draws a dagger from a pocket in his jerkin. You must fight him.

GREMLIN                 SKILL 4                 STAMINA 4

During each Attack Round you must reduce your Attack Strength by 3 because of your cramped fighting position. If you win, turn to 110.

## 194

The man smiles and takes off his mask, explaining that he wore it to protect him against the dust and not to hide the face of a robber. You sheathe your sword and relax a little. The man tells you that he is a hunter and that the best game in all the northern borderlands can be found on this grassy plain within Darkwood Forest. He says that his hounds were chasing a Wild Boar when they lost its scent and picked up that of the fox mistakenly. He warns you of some of the dangerous beasts that lurk in these parts and finally says, 'And if you are going to spend the night in Darkwood, you might need some of this.' He drops some belladonna into your hand and jumps back on his stallion. Then with a sudden blow of his horn, the dogs run off east. He turns and waves to you before galloping off in pursuit of his dogs. You put the belladonna into your backpack and set off west again. Turn to 208.

**195** *The creature is holding a large bone in his hand and grunts at you.*

**195**

You reach the top of the vine and scramble on to a wooden platform. A sheet made from leaves and ferns covers the entrance to a small covered living area. As you approach, the sheet is thrown back, and from behind it steps a large and hairy ape-like creature wearing only an animal-hide loin cloth. He is holding a large bone in his right hand and grunts at you. He is an APE MAN. You may:

| | |
|---|---|
| Draw your sword and attack him | Turn to **352** |
| Jump off the platform to the ground five metres below | Turn to **156** |

**196**

You step into the dark cavern with your sword drawn. The air is cold and moist. You hear a loud snoring and as your eyes adjust to the darkness you see the large bulk of a CAVE TROLL asleep in a large stone chair. His skin is brown and wrinkled, and he is wearing animal hides. A wooden club lies across his lap and a large leather bag hangs on the back of the stone chair. Will you:

| | |
|---|---|
| Creep up and take the leather bag while the Cave Troll sleeps? | Turn to **376** |
| Take out the Net of Entanglement (if you have it) from your backpack? | Turn to **39** |
| Walk back to the junction and head north? | Turn to **25** |

## 197

If you possess a Potion of Anti-Poison, turn to **24**. If not, turn to **53**.

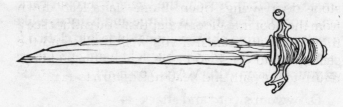

## 198

The ground is quite steep as the path wends its way into the hills. By the time you reach the top the sun is quite hot. All around in the distance you see the dark green circle of Darkwood Forest. Mist still hangs in the tall grasses behind you but ahead you see a valley floor bathed in sunlight. All is quiet. As you start down the far side of the hill you see a junction in the path. You may either continue north down the hill (turn to **278**) or head east along the new branch (turn to **87**).

## 199

To the left of the path you notice a large mud pool bubbling loudly. Steam rises from the thick bubbles breaking the surface of the mud. You may:

Throw a Gold Piece in the
   mud and make a wish       Turn to **134**
Rub some hot mud on to your
   wounds       Turn to **283**
Continue north along the path       Turn to **303**

**200**

You take the small silver key from out of your backpack and place it into the keyhole. It fits perfectly and you give it a turn. The lock clicks and the stone door swings open. Stone stairs lead down from the door into gloomy depths. You cannot see a thing down the stairs. If you wish to descend the stairs, turn to **351**. If you wish to leave the building, return to the path and head north, turn to **112**.

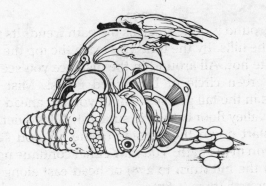

**201**

If you have not done so already, you may try to open the wooden chest – turn to **389**. Alternatively you may leave the alcove to climb further up the steps – turn to **88**.

**202**

The ears of the Catwoman are pierced by two gold studs. They are worth 5 Gold Pieces each and you put them into your backpack. You set off east along the twisting path – turn to **355**.

**204** *Beyond the bridge are the small cottages and wooden huts of a village.*

## 203

As you start to speak the Goblin looks up and smiles. Then he starts to metamorphose before your eyes. He becomes taller and turns green. A large spiny tail extends from his back, his arms thicken and his hands grow sharp claws. His face distorts and becomes reptilian with red eyes, a wide mouth and dozens of razor-sharp teeth. He is not a Goblin but a SHAPE CHANGER, and you must fight him.

SHAPE CHANGER     SKILL 10     STAMINA 10

If you win, turn to 373.

## 204

The path leads through the field to a stone bridge over a clear stream. Beyond the bridge are the small cottages and wooden huts of a village. A sign on the bridge reads 'Stonebridge'. You cross the bridge and see two old dwarfs with long white beards standing by a cottage looking at you. Do you have the hammer head and handle with the letter G inscribed in them? If you do, turn to **400**. If you possess neither or only one of these items, turn to **381**.

### 205

Each Pygmy has a small, leather pouch hung around his neck. You find 3 Gold Pieces in each. You take the gold and return to the path to continue your northwards journey. Turn to **92**.

### 206

Suddenly off the path to your left you hear cries for help. If you wish to go to the aid of the person in trouble, turn to **253**. If you would rather ignore the cries and continue your journey north, turn to **187**.

### 207

You step over the body of the Ape Man and enter his living area. Animal bones and rotting fruit litter the floor. The Ape Man's bed is made of moss and lichen and seems to be crawling with bugs. You shudder and step back out on to the platform. You then notice a copper bracelet around the Ape Man's wrist. If you want to put it on your own wrist, turn to **302**. If you would rather climb down the vine to the path, and carry on walking northwards, turn to **109**.

### 208

You soon arrive at a crossroads. The way south leads back to the forest so you decide to ignore it. You may either keep going west (turn to **99**) or head north (turn to **291**).

### 209

As you enter the hut the big man smiles. He looks pleased to see you and starts to speak in a deep voice. 'Welcome stranger. My name is Quin and I earn my living by my arms. Would you care for a little wager perhaps at arm wrestling?' If you wish to accept the challenge, turn to **28**. If you wish to decline his offer, you politely refuse and return to the junction in the path – turn to **349**.

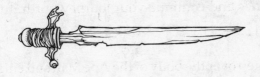

### 210

The men curse and jump up and down in anger at having missed you. They start to argue and push each other around. They seem to forget all about you. If you want to attack the WILD HILL MEN, turn to **43**. If you want to walk past them along the path while they are still arguing, turn to **188**.

### 211

You take the small bottle labelled Potion of Anti-Poison from your backpack and gulp down the contents. The pain in your stomach gradually fades away and you relax. There does not appear to be much sense in staying here any longer and you walk over to the steps on the far wall. Turn to **293**.

**212** You see four small humanoids wearing leather armour and carrying long spears.

## 212

Inside the alcove you see four more of the small humanoids. But these wear leather armour and carry long spears. They move to attack you and you are forced to fight the CLONE WARRIORS. They come at you one at a time:

|  | SKILL | STAMINA |
|---|---|---|
| First CLONE WARRIOR | 5 | 5 |
| Second CLONE WARRIOR | 6 | 4 |
| Third CLONE WARRIOR | 5 | 6 |
| Fourth CLONE WARRIOR | 6 | 5 |

If you win, turn to **321**. You may *Escape* by running out of the alcove and up the steps. Turn to **107**.

## 213

The path twists and turns between the trees and bushes, and then comes to another junction. You realize that the way south leads back to the valley and so you decide to ignore it and head north – turn to **306**.

## 214

You reach into your backpack and uncork the small bottle containing the healing potion. The pain in your leg is agonizing but rapidly dies down as the potion takes effect. Soon your leg is fully mended and you are able to stand on your feet. Your eyes are now accustomed to the dark and you see that the tunnel is only one metre high and you must crawl along on your hands and knees to explore it. Turn to **69**.

**215**

Inside the barrel you find a heavy iron shield. If you wish to take it with you, turn to **248**. If you do not wish to touch it, turn to **201**.

**216**

The path leads along a ridge of the hill and ends at another junction. You see that the way south leads back to the river, so you decide to head north again. Turn to **278**.

**217**

You walk around the lifeless bulk of the worm to examine the contents of its lair. There are several skeletons, perhaps those belonging to other unfortunate adventurers. By the side of one of them you find a leather backpack. Inside the backpack you find 4 Gold Pieces and a small, corked bottle containing a colourless liquid. If you wish to drink the contents of the bottle, turn to **262**. If you would rather leave the dark cavern and scramble back up to the path again taking just the gold with you, turn to **337**.

**218**

You curse as you wonder who set this infernal trap. After ten minutes you hear footsteps and begin to panic, making frantic swaying movements in the air trying to free your foot from the noose. Then a small boy dressed in green leather shorts and green shirt appears. He is chewing on what looks like a chicken bone. He walks underneath you, looks up and smiles, saying, 'Ha, ha, somebody's caught in the Ogre's tree trap.' You ask him politely to pass you your sword.

'That will cost you 5 Gold Pieces – or perhaps you have a nice magical item for me?' he says, eyes widening.

You are in no position to argue and must give the boy the gold or one of your magical items (if you have any). Make the necessary deduction on your *Adventure Sheet*. The small boy then passes you your sword and runs away down the path. You cut the rope holding your foot and fall heavily to the ground. You get to your feet and brush the dirt from your clothes. To continue northwards, turn to **274**.

**219**

You notice that the small dart that protrudes from the Bear's chest is made of silver. Its value is 5 Gold Pieces and you may put it in your backpack if you wish. Add 1 LUCK point for your discovery. You now return to the path and head north (turn to **300**).

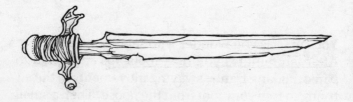

**220**

Walking along the narrow path you notice a big old tree to your left with a large hole in its trunk just above head height. If you wish to reach up to put your hand into the hole, turn to **275**. If you would rather continue walking north, turn to **115**.

**221**

The valley floor is covered with lush green grass and is very flat. You soon arrive at another junction in the path. You may either continue west (turn to **378**) or head north again (turn to **199**).

**222**

There is no escaping the poisonous gas cloud which has enveloped you. Your lungs feel as if they are bursting and you are forced to inhale. Reduce your STAMINA score by the amount of one die roll. If you are still alive you see the cloud drift away at last and you are able to breathe freely again. There does not seem to be much point in staying here any longer and you walk over to the steps on the far wall (turn to **293**).

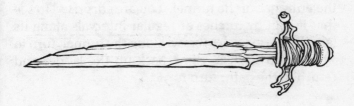

**223**

The jewel hanging round your neck starts to glow. Perhaps Arragon is not all that he says he is. You draw your sword and challenge him. The expression on Arragon's face changes from confidence to fear. He then apologizes for being so aggressive but explains that these lands are filled with bandits and murderers and he has to protect himself by pretending to be a wizard of supreme power. He begs forgiveness and offers you 5 Gold Pieces if you will leave him in peace and tell nobody of his disguise. You accept his offer and leave his cottage. You walk back to the junction in the passage and head north (turn to **150**).

## 224

One of the Death Hawks has a silver band around one of its legs. It has an inscription on it which reads 'Death awaits you'. You decide to leave the silver band and head quickly west (turn to 332).

## 225

You curse and pull yourself out of the water on to the entrance of the tunnel. You are surprised to see that it is lit by torches at regular intervals along its length. If you wish to crawl along the tunnel, turn to 135. If you wish to climb back up the ladder and return to the path, turn to 362.

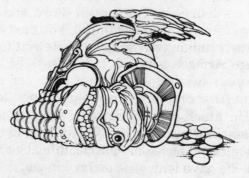

## 226

To the right of the path you hear voices arguing in a strange language coming through the trees. If you wish to step off the path to investigate, turn to 29. If you would rather ignore the voices and press on north along the path, turn to 254.

## 227

The creature about to attack you with its claws is a GHOUL.

GHOUL                SKILL 9                STAMINA 7

It has the ability to paralyse you if it scores four separate wounds on you during this battle. If you defeat the Ghoul, turn to **312**. If it kills you or paralyses you, turn to **2**.

## 228

The pit is circular, with smooth sides, and you are weak from your fall. You reach into your backpack and pull out the brown leather boots. They are very light on your feet. You crouch down and in one mighty leap you are out of the pit. You dust yourself off and continue your walk north down the gorge. Turn to **255**.

## 229

As you touch the wooden box, the lid flies up without your having to lift it. From out of the box leaps a tiny green-skinned creature with a large head. He has a long nose and pointed ears and his clothes are made of sacking. You are taken by surprise and the GREMLIN tries to stab you with his dagger. *Test your Luck*. If you are Lucky, you manage to dodge the thrusting blade (turn to **165**). If you are Unlucky, the blade sinks into your thigh (turn to **45**).

**230** *An Ogre walks slowly over to a wicker cage with a bowl of water in his great hand.*

Slowly you peer into the cave and see the huge shape of an OGRE walking slowly over to a wicker cage with a bowl of water in his great hand. He is dressed in animal furs and carries a stone club in his belt. There appears to be a small creature jumping around inside the cage. You may:

| | |
|---|---|
| Pick up a rock and throw it at the Ogre | Turn to 137 |
| Rush in and attack the Ogre with your sword | Turn to 290 |
| Leave the cave and continue up the path | Turn to 358 |

The path twists and turns and then makes a sudden sharp turn to the west. Following the new course you are aware of squawking in the trees all around you. You hear the flapping of wings and look up to see three large birds swooping down on you. Their beaks and talons look razor-sharp. You only have a second in which to draw your sword to defend yourself against the DEATH HAWKS.

| | SKILL | STAMINA |
|---|---|---|
| First DEATH HAWK | 4 | 4 |
| Second DEATH HAWK | 4 | 3 |
| Third DEATH HAWK | 5 | 4 |

Fight them one at a time and if you win, turn to 224. You may escape by running west along the path. Turn to 332.

## 232

You bend down over the lifeless body of the mad Goblin and examine the rod around its neck. The rod is made of ebony and there is a screw thread at one end. You are excited to see the letter G neatly inscribed at the other end of what must be the handle of the dwarfish war-hammer. You put your find in your backpack. Add 1 LUCK point. If you wish to search through the contents of the cave, turn to 263. If you want to leave the cave and continue northwards, turn to 358.

## 233

To the right of the path you see a stone well with a bucket and turning handle. If you wish to take a closer look at the well, turn to 17. If you would rather continue your walk west, turn to 238.

## 234

You arrive back at the junction in the path. Ignoring the way south you head west. Turn to 382.

## 235

You reach quickly into your backpack and pull out the small corked bottle containing the potion. You gulp down the liquid. Calm spreads through your body despite the chaos all around you. Suddenly the hut collapses and crashes to the ground. You decide it is time to get out of this place and run back to the path to head north. Add 1 LUCK point and turn to 149.

## 236

The path ends outside a stone cottage with a thatched roof. A plaque above the wooden door reads 'Arragon the Arch-Mage'. If you wish to enter the cottage, turn to **170**. If you would rather return to the junction in the path and head north, turn to **150**.

## 237

You land heavily on the ground, and you hear an ugly snapping sound. Pain shoots through your leg and you realize it is broken. Lose 2 LUCK points. Do you possess a Potion of Healing? If you do, turn to **214**. If you do not, turn to **304**.

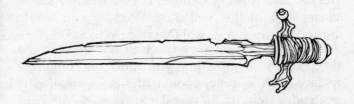

## 238

Walking west along the valley floor, you pass a junction in the path, which leads south and back into the hills. You decide to keep on walking west. Turn to **221**.

## 239

The path continues to cut its way through the dense undergrowth and you feel a little claustrophobic with the trees overhanging you on either side. After a while the path turns sharply to the left at a tree bearing strange fruit. If you wish to stop to eat some of the fruit, turn to **37**. If you wish to proceed north without stopping to eat, turn to **226**.

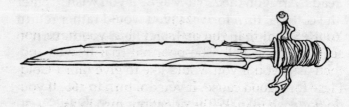

### 240

You gently prise the lid off the box, but as you do so, a yellow gas escapes and envelops your face. If you possess Nose Filters, turn to **338**. If not, turn to **169**.

### 241

As you wend your way through the trees in the direction of the growling, you suddenly come face to face with a huge, brown BEAR. A small dart protrudes from its chest and it looks mad with pain and rage. You draw your sword and prepare to fight.

BEAR                    SKILL 7                    STAMINA 8

If you win, turn to **219**.

### 242

Rummaging through some bedding in a chest of drawers you find an ingot of gold. It is worth 28 Gold Pieces. However it is very heavy and if you wish to take it with you, some other object from your backpack will have to be discarded. There is no other exit from the cave and you have to crawl back down the tunnel to the junction (turn to **121**).

### 243

You tell him that you are sorry, but you have not seen his brass bell. The poor old friar frowns and then asks you if you would like to give him 1 Gold Piece for a good cause. If you do, turn to **166**. If you do not wish to make the donation, turn to **33**.

### 244

The effects of the fever finally wear off and you gratefully fall asleep again. In the morning you collect your belongings and head north along the path to the hills. Turn to **198**.

### 245

Arriving on the valley floor you find that the path splits.

| | |
|---|---|
| To continue north | Turn to **163** |
| To go west | Turn to **233** |
| To go east | Turn to **393** |

### 246

The BANDIT woman takes the items from you and steps back to let you pass. You head north again and soon notice the trees beginning to thin out on either side of the path. Eventually the path leads out of the trees into a ploughed field. You are out of Dark-wood Forest! Turn to 204.

### 247

The loathsome Pterodactyl lies in a crumpled heap where it crashed to the floor after the fatal blow from your sword. Walking over to it you notice a yellow arrow painted on the grass beside the path, pointing west. If you wish to follow the arrow, turn to 3. If you wish to keep going north along the path, turn to 144.

### 248

You now possess an emperor's shield made long ago by a master armourer. Add 1 LUCK point. The shield will give you greater defence in all future battles. Should a creature wound you, throw one die. If you throw a 4, 5, or 6, its damage to you will be reduced by 1 point. If you have not done so already, you may now either try to open the wooden chest (turn to 389) or leave the alcove to climb further up the steps (turn to 88).

### 249

You look back into the strange cavern and see the humanoid clone workers continuing their labours in the fungi field. You shake your head in disbelief and run up the last few steps to the hole in the cavern roof. Turn to **164**.

### 250

The vase drops to the ground but does not break although cracks appear all over it. You begin to feel a vibration and then you notice cracks appearing all over the porch and the sides of the hut. The vibrations become stronger – your whole body starts to tremble and your head feels as if it is about to explode. Lose 2 STAMINA points. If you are still alive, turn to **82**.

### 251

As you draw your sword the Centaur reaches for his bow and arrows. Before you can reach him he lets fly an arrow straight at you. Roll two dice. If the number rolled is less than or equal to your SKILL score, you manage to dodge the arrow; turn to **63** If the number rolled is greater than your SKILL score, you are unable to dodge the arrow which lodges itself into your shoulder. Lose 4 STAMINA points. If you are still alive, you pull the arrow, painfully, out of your shoulder; turn to **260**.

### 252

You arrive at a four-way junction in the path. South leads back to the forest so you discount that option. If you wish to head north, turn to **309**. If you wish to continue east, turn to **72**.

**253** *A man dressed in long dark robes has his foot caught in a rusted rabbit snare.*

### 253

Clambering over the gnarled roots of the old trees you head in the direction of the cries. After a few minutes you see a man dressed in long dark robes with his foot caught in a rusted rabbit snare. His face is masked by the robes and only his dark brown eyes are visible. If you want to help the man free his foot from the snare, turn to **344**. If you decide against helping him, return to the path and head north – turn to **187**.

### 254

Further along the narrow path you hear a deep growl to your left in the trees. If you want to see what creature is growling, turn to **241**. If you prefer to ignore the creature and continue north along the path, turn to **300**.

### 255

Continuing down the gorge you see the handle of a sword sticking out from a large rock by the side of the path. If you wish to try to pull the sword free from the rock, turn to **182**. If you wish to continue walking down the gorge, turn to **334**.

### 256

Climbing down the ladder you do not notice that a rung is missing. You slip and lose your footing. *Test your Luck*. If you are Lucky, you manage to hang on to the ladder with your hands; turn to **122**. If you are Unlucky, you fall off the ladder and plunge to the water below; turn to **295**.

## 257

Inside the backpack you find some elven bread which will restore 4 STAMINA points if you eat it. Add 1 LUCK point and turn to **31**.

## 258

You reach into your backpack and pull out the tiny brass flute. You have a strange feeling that you must play it now, before the enraged Wyvern. As you do, a soft and gentle sound plays out from the flute and a quizzical look appears on the Wyvern's face. Its mouth closes and its eyelids start to droop. You are playing a magical Flute of Dragonsleep and the Wyvern is powerless to resist its soothing song. Slowly the Wyvern slumps to the ground and is soon fast asleep. Turn to **305**.

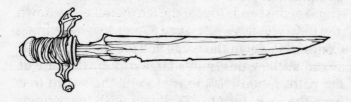

## 259

You feel a burning sensation inside your body as you sink into a raging fever. You may be about to change into a Werewolf yourself! Lose 3 STAMINA points and *Test your Luck* if you are still alive. If the number rolled is equal to or less than your LUCK score, the fever dies down – turn to **244**. If the number rolled is greater than your LUCK score, the fever continues to grip your body and you are horrified to see thick brown hair appearing on the back of your hands. Shock causes you to lose 2 additional STAMINA points. If you are still alive, turn to **19**.

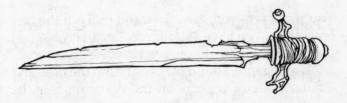

#### 260

On seeing that the arrow has not killed you the Centaur rears up on to his hind legs and then charges you at a gallop. You have to jump back to avoid being run down. He thunders past you in a cloud of dust and stops some ten metres away down the path you have just come along. Maybe fighting the noble Centaur is not such a good idea after all. You sheathe your sword and decide to wade across the river. Turn to **178**.

#### 261

You follow the huffing and puffing old man in his tattered robes up the spiral staircase to a large room at the top of the tower. Shelves, cupboards and cabinets line the walls, all filled with bottles, jars, weapons, armour and all manner of strange artefacts. Yaztromo shuffles past the general clutter and slumps down in an old oak chair. He reaches into his top pocket and pulls out a fragile pair of gold-rimmed spectacles. Placing these on his nose, he picks up a piece of slate and chalk from a table next to his chair and begins to write frantically. He then hands you the slate.

| ITEM | COST |
|------|------|
| Potion of Healing | 3 Gold Pieces |
| Potion of Plant Control | 2 Gold Pieces |
| Potion of Stillness | 3 Gold Pieces |
| Potion of Insect Control | 2 Gold Pieces |
| Potion of Anti-Poison | 2 Gold Pieces |
| Holy Water | 3 Gold Pieces |
| Ring of Light | 3 Gold Pieces |
| Boots of Leaping | 2 Gold Pieces |
| Rope of Climbing | 3 Gold Pieces |
| Net of Entanglement | 3 Gold Pieces |
| Armband of Strength | 3 Gold Pieces |
| Glove of Missile Dexterity | 2 Gold Pieces |
| Rod of Water-finding | 2 Gold Pieces |
| Garlic Buds | 2 Gold Pieces |
| Headband of Concentration | 3 Gold Pieces |
| Fire Capsules | 3 Gold Pieces |
| Nose Filters | 3 Gold Pieces |

He tells you that all the instructions for use are written clearly on the labels attached to the items, together with their suggested use. He sighs and tells you that unfortunately the magic in the items only works once, but they are the best you can buy for the money.

If you decide to buy any of the items, pay for them by reducing the amount of Gold on your *Adventure Sheet* and add the items to the relevant sections on it. Yaztromo then asks you the reason for the purchase of the items, and you tell him your story and your decision to continue the quest of the luckless Bigleg. 'Ah yes,' Yaztromo says slowly, rubbing his chin, 'I heard that the good dwarfs of Stonebridge had lost their fabled war-hammer. Without it, their king is unable to arouse his people, despite the fact that the hill trolls threaten their village. Rumour has it that an envious king of another village of dwarfs sent an eagle to Stonebridge to steal the hammer, which it managed to do. But as it flew back over Darkwood, it was attacked by death hawks and the hammer dropped into the forest and was lost. Apparently, two forest goblins found the hammer but could not decide who was to keep it. They wrestled for hours but gave up. Then they discovered that the handle unscrewed from the head, and the argument was settled. One kept the head, the other kept the handle. Then they parted, each happy with his new treasure. Who knows if they still have them. So I'm afraid your problems are doubled. I can tell you that the head is made of bronze and the handle is made of polished ebony. Both head and handle have the letter G inscribed on them. Your task is not easy. Good luck.'

You thank Yaztromo and leave the room by the spiral staircase. Turn to **177**.

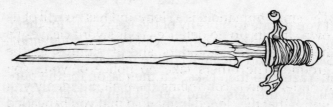

**262**

You look at the bottle in your hand and then quickly gulp down its contents. You wait several seconds for some reaction, but nothing happens. However, when you come to pick up your sword, which you had put down to examine the backpack, a surge of confidence runs through your body. The liquid is a Potion of Weapon Skill which will allow you to add 1 point to future dice rolls when computing your own Attack Strength during combat. Its effect will last for your next two combat encounters. Taking the gold, you scramble up out of the earthen cavern to the path above and continue your journey northwards. Turn to **337**.

**263**

There is not much of interest to be found in the cave. A straw bed, stone jars, a table and a chair are all that is immediately visible, but on a stone shelf above the bed, a small silver box catches your eye. If you want to open the silver box, turn to **126**. If you would rather leave the cave and go north up the path without the silver box, turn to **358**.

## 264

The small humanoid is a clone and has no will of its own. It puts up no defence. Your sword cleaves its head from its shoulders and it slumps to the ground. The others take no notice of you. You wonder who is controlling them all. Suddenly you notice that the cloned humanoid that you beheaded is dissolving into a pool of purple liquid and a new fungus sprouts out of the soil. As the fungus rises, the purple pool drains into the ground. The fungus has a purple top which moves round to face you. You may:

| | |
|---|---|
| Stay to watch the purple-topped fungus | Turn to **367** |
| Head towards the green-topped fungus | Turn to **189** |
| Head towards the red-topped fungus | Turn to **282** |

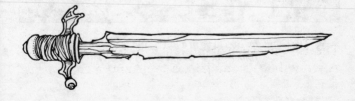

**265** *The Giant appears to be in a hurry and is crashing through the undergrowth as if it weren't there.*

## 265

The thumping and crashing gets louder and suddenly you see a huge leg appear in front of you. Looking up you see that the leg belongs to a man some five metres tall. He is wearing brown canvas clothing and fur boots. He appears to be in a hurry and is crashing through the undergrowth as though it isn't there. He is a FOREST GIANT. On seeing you his eyes widen and he raises his great wooden club. You must fight him.

FOREST GIANT     SKILL 9     STAMINA 9

If you win, turn to **356**.

## 266

Quin explains that he will wager some Dust of Levitation against an item or coins to the value of 10 Gold Pieces. You sit down at the table opposite him. You put your elbow on to the table and lock hands with him. His grip is like an iron vice and his dark slanted eyes look confident. His biceps bulge and he gives the signal for the contest to begin. Roll two dice. If the number rolled is less than or equal to your SKILL score, you manage with great effort to push his arm down slightly. He is strong and will not give in easily. You must roll successfully against your SKILL score two more times before you are able to push his arm down on to the table top. If you are successful, turn to **354**. If any of the three rolls exceeds your SKILL score, your arm gives way to Quin's strength and collapses on to the table top – turn to **129**.

## 267

The path leads to a large cave entrance and does not appear to go any further east. If you want to enter the cave, turn to **196**. If you would rather return to the junction and go north, turn to **25**.

## 268

You reach quickly into your backpack and pull out the Garlic Buds. The Vampire Bats close in on you but veer away at the last second, screeching loudly. They hover above you, eager to drink your blood, but the garlic keeps them at bay. Eventually they fly off in search of some other prey. Leaving the garlic by your side, you settle down to sleep again. In the morning you collect your belongings and head north along the path. Turn to **119**.

## 269

You shout at two humanoids who are tending a patch of green-topped fungi. They ignore you, continuing with their work. You grab hold of a fungus top, breaking a piece off, and start to eat. It tastes good and adds strength to your body. You gain 4 STAMINA points. There does not seem much sense in staying here any longer and you walk over to the steps on the far wall. Turn to **293**.

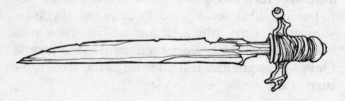

## 270

The tunnel ends at a cave entrance. On entering the cave you see that the roof is no higher than the tunnel and you are unable to stand up. The cave is the lair of an intelligent creature, for it contains small pieces of furniture. There is a wooden box just over a metre in length at the back of the cave. If you wish to lift the lid of the box, turn to **229**. If you wish to turn round and return to the junction in the tunnel, turn to **121**.

## 271

You approach the Gnome with your arm extended offering to shake his hand, an offer which he accepts with a doubtful look on his face. You then tell him of your quest, how you met poor Bigleg and why you decided to help the dwarfs of Stonebridge. You ask him if he has any information which might help you. He replies that he does not care much for dwarfs but he does have some information which might be of use to you. However, that information will cost you either 5 Gold Pieces or an item of treasure from your backpack. If you wish to pay the greedy Gnome for his information, turn to **297**. If you cannot afford to, or do not wish to pay him, you tell him what you think of him and set off west along the path – turn to **67**.

## 272

That is the last time you are going to do anybody a favour for some time! Returning to the path you head north again. Turn to **394**.

## 273

You take the medallion from the neck of the fallen Gremlin. It is made of gold and is worth 9 Gold Pieces. There is nothing else of use or value in the cave. There is no other exit from the cave and you must crawl back down the tunnel to the junction – turn to **296**.

## 274

You notice a knotted vine hanging down to the ground from a tree on your left. You look up and see a roughly made tree house amid the branches. If you want to climb up the vine to the tree house, turn to **195**. If you wish to continue walking north, turn to **109**.

## 275

You put your hand slowly into the dark hole. It comes into contact with something cold and hard. It feels like a metal bowl. As you start to lift it out of the hole you wince with pain as the sharp teeth of some small creature suddenly bite into your arm. You pull your arm out quickly, hanging on to your discovery. Blood drips to the ground from your wound. Lose 1 STAMINA point. You see that you have not found a metal bowl after all. It is a bronze helmet and it looks about your size. Will you:

Try on the helmet? Turn to **179**

Discard it and continue
  north? Turn to **115**

As you step back to attack the masked rider, the largest of the four dogs leaps at you and you are forced to fight it first.

| HUNTING DOG | SKILL 7 | STAMINA 6 |
|---|---|---|

If you defeat the Hunting Dog, you must now fight the other three dogs and their master in pairs. Both members of a pair will have a separate attack on you in each Attack Round, but you must choose which of the two you will fight. Attack your nominated target as in a normal battle. Against the other you will throw for your Attack Strength in the normal way, but you will not wound it if your Attack Strength is greater – you must just count this as though you have parried its blow. Of course if its Attack Strength is greater, it will have wounded you in the normal way.

|  |  | SKILL | STAMINA |
|---|---|---|---|
| First pair: | HUNTING DOG | 6 | 6 |
|  | HUNTING DOG | 5 | 6 |
| Second pair: | HUNTING DOG | 6 | 5 |
|  | MASKED MAN | 8 | 7 |

If you win, turn to **62**.

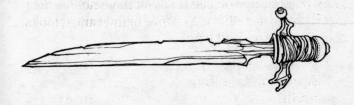

**277** *Suddenly, a branch whips out and knocks you to the ground.*

## 277

The path continues east for some distance and then turns sharply north, narrowing slightly. The trees seem to crowd in on the path even more than usual and a tingling down your spine tells you something is not right. Suddenly a branch from one of the trees to your right whips out and knocks you to the ground. Lose 1 STAMINA point. You stagger to your feet to see that the tree has moved on to the path, blocking your way. The tree is old, with thick, cracked bark. You can just make out its hidden eyes and mouth in the middle of its trunk and realize you have been attacked by a TREEMAN. You may:

| | |
|---|---|
| *Escape* by running back to the junction | Turn to **234** |
| Fight the Treeman | Turn to **114** |

## 278

The path runs through a narrow gorge between two hills. You feel vulnerable and draw your sword, expecting to be ambushed at any moment. Unfortunately, because you are concentrating on watching the sides of the gorge, you do not see a small patch of leaves and branches on the path ahead. Your foot goes right through the thin covering of a bear trap, and you plunge four metres to the bottom of a rocky pit. To add to your misfortune, a wooden stake with a sharp tip points out of the centre of the pit. *Test your Luck*. If you are Lucky, you manage to avoid landing on the wooden stake, but fall heavily to the floor. Lose 2 STAMINA points and turn to **319** if you are still alive. If you are Unlucky, the point of the stake pierces your leg as you land. Lose 2 STAMINA points for the fall, and a further 2 STAMINA points for injury to your leg. If you are still alive turn to **319**.

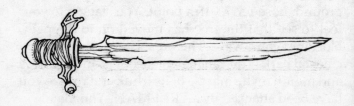

### 279

Treat all the items in your backpack as single objects, including each Gold Piece. Make the necessary deductions to your Equipment List and turn to **246**.

### 280

Your walk west is arduous but uneventful. You pass two branches off the path leading south which you ignore. Eventually you arrive at a junction. Again ignoring the way south you head north; turn to **306**.

### 281

You arrive at a crossroads. South leads back up into the hills so you decide against that option. If you wish to head north, turn to **163**. If you wish to continue east, turn to **393**.

### 282

The red-topped fungi are being tended by three of the humanoids. If you want to eat some of the fungus, turn to **16**. If you wish to leave the cavern by the steps on the far wall, turn to **293**.

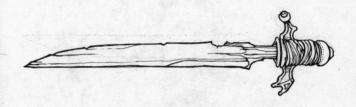

### 283

Your wounds heal before your eyes due to the magical properties of the mud. Add 4 STAMINA points to your score. Feeling much better you set off north again along the path; turn to **303**.

### 284

You soon arrive at another junction in the tunnel. If you wish to head north, turn to **81**. If you wish to head south, turn to **270**.

**285** *You hear soft footsteps and sniffing, followed by a low growl.*

## 285

You have been asleep for about an hour when the noise of deep growling wakes you up. You stand up without making a noise and grab your sword. You wait and listen. There is a full moon in the sky and the light casts eerie shadows all around. You hear soft footsteps and sniffing followed by another low growl. Then a shape which looks like a man steps out of the shadows to your right; as he gets closer you see that his chest, arms and face are covered with thick brown hair and long teeth protrude from his mouth. He is a WEREWOLF and you must fight him.

WEREWOLF                 SKILL 8                 STAMINA 9

If you defeat him, turn to **388**.

## 286

As you raise your sword to make the first blow, the creature starts to metamorphose before your eyes. He becomes taller and turns green. A large spiny tail extends from his back, his arms thicken and his hands grow sharp claws. His face distorts and becomes reptilian with red eyes and a wide mouth housing dozens of razor-sharp teeth. He is not a Goblin but a SHAPE CHANGER, and you must fight him.

SHAPE CHANGER           SKILL 10               STAMINA 10

If you win, turn to **373**.

**287**

Outside the cave you stop to take a quick look inside the leather bag. You find 5 Gold Pieces and a small brass bell. You put these in your backpack and run back to the junction in the path and head north. Turn to **25**.

**288**

Walking down the hill path you see the valley floor stretching out ahead and beyond that the sinister wall of trees – Darkwood! On the other side of the trees lies Stonebridge, your journey's end. As you reach the foot of the hills you see many large boulders lying around on either side of the path. You are amazed to see one of the larger ones gently rocking from side to side like a leaf in a breeze. If you wish to investigate the boulder, turn to **84**. If you would rather head north into the valley, turn to **245**.

**289**

The narrow, overgrown path continues to weave its way through the crowded forest. Strange animal cries echo through the trees. It's not long before you arrive at another junction in the path. If you wish to continue westwards, turn to **76**. If you wish to turn north, turn to **147**.

**290**

You draw your sword as you enter the cave. The Ogre throws down the wooden bowl and lifts the large stone club from his belt. He grunts and lopes towards you. Prepare for battle.

OGRE           SKILL 8          STAMINA 12

If you win, turn to **385**. You may *Escape* by running back to the path to head north. Turn to **358**.

### 291

As you walk further northwards across the plain, the grass gradually becomes shorter and the ground starts to rise gently. Ahead you hear the roar of crashing water. Soon you reach the bank of a wide river split on two levels. To your right the water is calm and slow-moving but in front of you it tumbles noisily down a great waterfall to a gorge below where the river narrows and runs quickly west over rocks and boulders. Steps lead down by the side of the waterfall to the bottom of the gorge, although it is difficult to see where they end because of the spray thrown up. Across the river you see the path heading north into the distance. A small wooden boat is tied to a post to your right where the river is calm. Will you:

| | |
|---|---|
| Walk down the steps to the base of the waterfall? | Turn to **335** |
| Row the wooden boat across the river? | Turn to **145** |

### 292

The light from the candle casts eerie shadows around the room. In the yellow light you see the face

**294** *The room does not appear to have been lived in for months.*

of an old man carved into the stone slab top of the box. Then you notice the leg of a skeleton protruding from the shadows in the far corner of the room. You walk over to the skeleton to inspect it. The skeleton is small and the skull has sharp, protruding teeth. It could be the skeleton of either a goblin or an orc. You walk over to the stone box. The slab on top looks as if it could be moved. If you wish to try to lift the stone slab, turn to **95**. If you wish to ignore the slab, return to the path and head north; turn to **112**.

### 293

The steps are made of stone, chiselled into the wall of the cavern. They are wet from the slime which drips down the walls. You see that there are three alcoves leading off the steps into the cavern wall at various intervals up to the roof. They are each three metres high. You climb the steps and peer into the gloom of the first alcove, where you see a barrel and a wooden chest. You may:

| | |
|---|---|
| Look inside the barrel | Turn to **215** |
| Try to open the wooden chest | Turn to **389** |
| Continue climbing up the steps | Turn to **88** |

### 294

The hut consists of one room containing a fireplace, a wooden bed, a table with two chairs, a washing bowl, a wooden chest and shelves crammed end to end with birds' eggs. There is a lot of dust on the floor and the room does not appear to have been lived in for months. Will you:

Rummage through the fireplace?     Turn to **106**
Open the wooden chest?               Turn to **175**
Leave the room and carry on
    northwards?                          Turn to **288**

### 295

You smash your head on the side of the well as you fall. Are you wearing a helmet? If you are, turn to **225**. If you are not, turn to **30**.

### 296

Back at the junction you may either crawl south back to the well (turn to **398**) or continue west (turn to **284**).

### 297

As he accepts his payment, the Gnome smiles and tells you that he saw the skeleton of a Goblin inside a stone crypt. Perhaps it was the skeleton of one of the two Goblins who you are looking for, perhaps not. He says that the crypt is somewhere north in the forest but exactly where, he's not sure. You are annoyed that the Gnome does not have any more information and set off west again at a fast pace – turn to **67**.

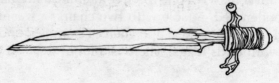

## 298

You have been asleep for about an hour when a terrifying howl wakes you up with a start. It seems to be coming from the west some distance away. You look up to see a full moon in the night sky. While looking up you suddenly notice a large black shape moving in the branches above you. You forget about the howling and leap to your feet, grabbing your sword at the same time as a GIANT SPIDER drops to the ground beside you. Its massive rounded body moves slowly towards you on black spiny legs. Not wishing to leave all your possessions you are forced to fight.

GIANT SPIDER     SKILL 7     STAMINA 8

If you win, turn to **140**.

## 299

You run as fast as you can towards the noise of the water with a long trail of KILLER BEES right behind you. Soon you reach the bank of a river and, with no time to think, you dive straight in. You hold your breath as long as you can and stay under water. When you surface again the Killer Bees have gone. You drag yourself out of the water and start to dry yourself out. Examining the contents of your backpack, you are dismayed to discover that all your Provisions have dissolved in the water. You look around and see that the path continues north over the river via a rickety old wooden bridge. If you wish to cross the river via the bridge, turn to **65**. If you do not want to trust the bridge and would rather swim across the river, turn to **75**.

### 300

Daylight appears through the trees in great white shafts on either side of the path. The forest is thinning out. Soon the path leads out of the trees on to a large plain with tall grasses. Beyond, you see rising ground leading to low hills. A new branch off the path leads west. Will you:

| | |
|---|---|
| Continue north? | Turn to **138** |
| Go west? | Turn to **331** |

### 301

You search through the pockets of the Hobgoblins and find 3 Gold Pieces, a tiny brass flute and two maggot-ridden biscuits. There is also a necklace made of mouse skulls around one of their necks. If you require any of these items, add them to your Equipment List. Turn to **157**.

### 302

You twist the bracelet into place on your wrist. A powerful feeling surges through your arm and makes you jump. Your arm feels strong. You now possess a Bracelet of Skill which will allow you to add 1 point to all future dice rolls when computing your own Attack Strength during combat as long as you wear it. Note this on your Equipment List. You now climb down the vine and continue northwards along the path. Turn to **109**.

## 303

High in the sky you see a large flying creature. It is certainly bigger than any bird you have ever seen. As it comes closer you draw your sword. It screeches loudly and you can see its long head and mouth full of sharp teeth. Its green skin is reptilian and its wings span some five metres. There is nowhere to take cover on the valley floor and you must fight the PTERODACTYL swooping down on you.

PTERODACTYL       SKILL 7        STAMINA 8

If you win, turn to **247**.

## 304

Your leg is going to take a long time to heal. You find two branches on the floor and strap them to your broken leg with the leather belt from around your waist. You sit back and begin your rest. You will have to consume five portions of your Provisions before being strong enough to move on. If you do not have five portions of Provisions left, you will die of starvation. If you survive, reduce your SKILL score by 2 points due to your disability. Your eyes are now well accustomed to the dark and you see that the tunnel is only one metre high. You must crawl along on your hands and knees to explore it. Turn to **69**.

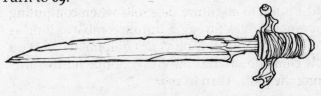

### 305

You walk round the motionless Wyvern and start to rummage through its lair and surrounding debris. You find a gauntlet made of plate iron, a throwing knife, 10 Gold Pieces and a gold ring. You put the knife and the Gold Pieces in your backpack. Will you:

| | |
|---|---|
| Try on the gauntlet? | Turn to 374 |
| Try on the gold ring? | Turn to 133 |
| Leave these items and head north along the path? | Turn to 360 |

### 306

Amidst the trees to the left of the path you see a small stone building covered with ivy and moss. If you wish to examine the building, turn to 391. If you wish to carry on north along the path, turn to 112.

### 307

The small man wakes up with a start, loses his balance and falls off the mushroom. He curses as he lands on the ground but jumps back on to the mushroom shouting, 'Who did that? Who did that?' He looks at you and frowns. You may either attack the GNOME (turn to 192) or attempt to start a conversation with him (turn to 271).

### 308

On eating some of the mushrooms you feel a great turmoil inside your body. You think you might be turning into a Shape Changer! At last you are relieved to feel the turmoil dying down – and you have not become a Shape Changer. But you have eaten Mix-Up Mushrooms – your SKILL score now becomes your LUCK score and your LUCK score becomes your SKILL score. Feeling a little odd you set off north again. Turn to **148**.

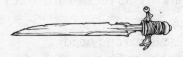

**309**

The path cuts through the grass which is about waist high. Although your visibility is good, you feel uneasy about any creatures which may be stalking you on either side. Suddenly, the grass to your left moves and two wooden tubes appear, pointing straight at you. They are blowpipes belonging to two PYGMIES who blow two darts at you. *Test your Luck* twice, once for each dart. If you are Lucky both times, neither of the darts hits you. Turn to **77**. If you are Unlucky, then either one or two darts will lodge into your neck. Turn to **197**.

**310**

The Cave Troll stands up and growls loudly. He is very annoyed at seeing an intruder in his cave and walks towards you swinging his club. You must fight him.

CAVE TROLL       SKILL 8       STAMINA 9

If you win, turn to **101**.

### 311

A search of their clothing and pouches reveals nothing of interest apart from 2 Gold Pieces, which you put in your backpack. You set off north again along the path and soon notice the trees beginning to thin out on either side of the path. Eventually the path leads out of the trees into a ploughed field. You are out of Darkwood Forest! Turn to **204**.

### 312

You step over the still corpse of the Ghoul and look inside the coffin. You see 25 Gold Pieces but are overjoyed to see another object that was being used as the Ghoul's head rest – a bronze hammer head with the letter G inscribed in it. You happily put your findings into your backpack and leave the crypt to return to the path and head north; turn to **112**.

### 313

There is not much of interest to be found in the cave. A straw bed, stone jars, a table and a chair are all the things that are immediately visible, but on a stone shelf above the bed, a small silver box catches your eye. If you want to open the silver box, turn to **240**. If you decide to ignore the silver box and walk over to the creature in the cage, turn to **85**. If you decide to leave the cave immediately without the silver box to continue your journey northwards, turn to **358**.

### 314

The ground is quite steep now as the path wends its way up into the hills. By the time you reach the top of the hill the sun is quite hot. All around in the distance you see the tight green circle of Darkwood Forest. Mist still hangs in the tall grasses behind you but ahead you see a valley floor bathed in sunlight. All is quiet. As you start down the far side of the hill, you notice a small wooden hut to the right of the path with its door slightly open. If you want to enter the hut, turn to **294**. If you wish to press on northwards, turn to **288**.

### 315

You open a rough wooden door and walk into the middle of a dingy hut. Will you:

| | |
|---|---|
| Talk to the old woman? | Turn to **42** |
| Draw your sword? | Turn to **342** |

### 316

Eventually you manage to get back to sleep but have a restless night. In the morning you collect your belongings and head north along the path into the hills. Turn to **198**.

**317** *Two tall, spindly creatures, clad in tattered cloth.*

## 317

You draw your sword and prepare to meet the owners of the arguing voices. Two tall, spindly creatures appear clad in tattered cloth, over which they wear chainmail jackets. They see you and instantly stop their argument. They are HOBGOB-LINS, and draw their swords to attack you.

|                  | SKILL | STAMINA |
|------------------|-------|---------|
| First HOBGOBLIN  | 6     | 6       |
| Second HOBGOBLIN | 5     | 7       |

If you win, turn to **301**. If you wish to *Escape* during the battle, you may do so by turning to **41**.

## 318

You jump into the thick undergrowth by the side of the path. Peering out from behind the leaves you see the massive legs of some gigantic man stomp past you along the path. Soon he is gone and you creep back out on to the path again and head north; turn to **231**.

## 319

Do you possess Boots of Leaping? If you do, turn to **228**. If you do not, turn to **14**.

## 320

You grab hold of the leg and pull down as hard as you can. A small green-skinned GREMLIN falls past you with a loud wail into the water. You seize your opportunity and climb up the ladder while the

Gremlin is floundering in the water. You climb out of the well and return to the path; turn to **362**.

## 321

As each Clone Warrior dies, it dissolves into a pool of coloured liquid on the rocky floor. Not wishing to stay in this dank and musty alcove any longer, you leave and climb further up the steps; turn to **107**.

## 322

The light from your ring pierces the murky depths of the tree trunk and the tunnel below. You see a gold medallion hanging from a silk ribbon within your reach on a wooden peg inside the trunk. It is worth 5 Gold Pieces and you put it in your backpack. The bottom of the tunnel is some five metres below. Do you possess a Rope of Climbing? If you do, turn to **94**. If you do not, turn to **380**.

## 323

Walking north you soon arrive at a junction in the path. You may:

| | |
|---|---|
| Continue north | Turn to **291** |
| Go west | Turn to **99** |
| Go east | Turn to **102** |

## 324

You walk round to the front of the hut and see a large blue vase standing on a small porch. There is nobody about. You open the door of the hut but there is nobody inside. The hut is also devoid of any furniture or objects. You walk outside again and inspect the blue vase. You look inside but, despite the sunlight, are unable to see beyond the rim. The vase is filled with an eerie blackness. You shake it and hear a rattling sound. You may:

| | |
|---|---|
| Drop the vase on the ground | Turn to 250 |
| Put your hand inside the vase | Turn to 161 |
| Ignore the vase and return to the path and head north | Turn to 149 |

### 325

You have been asleep for about an hour when the soft noise of fluttering wings wakes you up. You sit up and grab your sword, and in the light of the full moon you see three large shapes flying towards you. They look like large bats, but as they swoop in close you see the unmistakable fangs of VAMPIRE BATS. If you possess any Garlic Buds, turn to 268. If not, turn to 79.

### 326

Standing at the river's edge, there does not appear to be any way of crossing the river other than the boat. Turn to 145.

### 327

Inside you see stone stairs leading down from the door into gloomy depths. You cannot see a thing down the stairs. If you wish to descend the stairs, turn to 351. If you wish to leave the building, return to the path and head north, turn to 112.

## 328

Despite being made of hard oak, the chair is surprisingly comfortable. You start to eat but instead of feeling stronger you feel weaker. You are sitting in a Chair of Life Draining which drains 4 points from your STAMINA score despite eating a portion of your Provisions. If you are still alive you manage to climb slowly out of the chair and stagger northwards along the path. Turn to **118**.

## 329

Daylight appears through the trees on either side of the path as the forest thins out more. Soon the path leads out of the trees on to a large plain with tall grasses. Beyond you see rising ground leading to low hills. A new branch off the path leads east. Continuing your quest you may:

Keep on walking north        Turn to **180**
Go east        Turn to **252**

## 330

You have been asleep for about an hour when a terrifying howl wakes you up with a start. You put new wood on the glowing embers of the fire and urge it back to life. You notice that there is a full moon in the sky. With your back to the rocks and the fire in front of you, you stand and wait with sword drawn. Soon you are aware of being watched and then you see three pairs of eyes ahead of you glowing red by the light of the fire. Another howl pierces the night air, followed by deep growls.

Slowly the three pairs of eyes advance towards you. From out of the shadows step three WOLVES ready to leap on you. They attack you one at a time.

|  | SKILL | STAMINA |
|---|---|---|
| First WOLF | 7 | 7 |
| Second WOLF | 8 | 7 |
| Third WOLF | 7 | 9 |

If you win, turn to 116.

### 331

You soon arrive at another junction in the path. You see that the path leading south heads straight back into the forest and decide against it. Therefore, you may:

Continue west                        Turn to 124
Go north                                 Turn to 309

### 332

You soon arrive at another junction in the path. Looking at Bigleg's map you decide to head north again in the direction of Stonebridge, ignoring the narrow path which continues west. Turn to 103.

### 333

The crown fits perfectly on your head. The two Clone Warriors look up and stare in awe at you. With the crown on your head you hear talking in your mind and realize that the Clone Warriors are trying to communicate telepathically with you. They tell you that you are their new master and they require instructions. They ask you what should be done with the new crop of red-topped fungi. You decide that you do not want to be master of the Clone Warriors and workers and raise your hands to your head to remove the crown. With horror you see that the skin on your hands has withered and darkened dramatically. You try to take the crown off your head but it will not move. It is evil and has found a new host in you. Gradually your features change as you adopt the shape and colour of a Fire Demon. Your new destiny is determined and your adventure ends here.

## 334

Between the hills you see the flat green valley floor stretching out ahead and, beyond, a sinister wall of trees – Darkwood Forest! On the other side of the trees lies Stonebridge, your journey's end. Arriving on the valley floor, the path ends at a junction. If you want to head west, turn to **113**. If you want to head east, turn to **51**.

## 335

You walk down the slippery stone steps to the bottom of the waterfall. You look up and see a magnificent rainbow reflected in the spray. It is dark in the gorge and impossible to see through the wall of water where the steps end. If you wish to walk through the sheet of water, turn to **181**. If you wish to climb back up the stone steps, turn to **326**.

## 336

A pain starts in your stomach and slowly spreads through your body. If you have a Potion of Anti-Poison, turn to **21**. If you do not possess this item, turn to **108**.

## 337

At last the trees begin to thin out and shafts of sunlight beam down through the gaps on either side of the path. As the path widens you see a large cave entrance set a few yards back on the right. If you want to examine the cave, turn to **230**. If you want to continue northwards up the path, turn to **358**.

## 338

The gas is toxic and your eyes start to water. You hold your breath long enough to find the Nose Filters and slip them into place inside your nostrils. You inhale tentatively, but all is well. After a while, the gas cloud around your face fades away. You put the silver box into your backpack. If you want to walk over to the creature in the cage, turn to **85**. If you would rather leave the cave to continue your journey northwards, turn to **358**.

## 339

You soon reach the bank of a gently flowing river. You see that the path continues north over the river via a rickety old wooden bridge. If you wish to cross the river by the bridge, turn to **65**. If you do not want

**340** *A small man wearing an iron helmet and a chainmail coat sitting on a log.*

to trust the bridge and would rather swim across the river holding your backpack out of the water to keep the contents dry, turn to **75**.

### 340

Walking along the path you see a small man wearing an iron helmet and a chainmail coat sitting on a log by the side of the path. He is a DWARF and he does not look very pleased to see you. Will you:

| | |
|---|---|
| Try to start a conversation with him? | Turn to **141** |
| Draw your sword to attack him? | Turn to **347** |
| Push him off the log and run east along the path? | Turn to **59** |

### 341

The pain in your hand becomes almost unbearable but you still retain feeling in it. At the bottom of the vase your hand comes into contact with several objects. You grasp them and pull your hand quickly out of the vase. You are surprised to see no mark or sign of injury on your hand. You examine your treasure and find 5 Gold Pieces, a dragon's tooth, and a glass phial containing a Potion of Strength which will restore 5 STAMINA points whenever you decide to drink it. Add 1 LUCK point and return to the path to head north; turn to **149**.

### 342

As you draw your sword, the old woman's face changes from an expression of disinterest to that of anger. From a drawer in a nearby table she pulls out some dead flowers and proceeds to rub a few petals on her palms, filling the hut with a sweet smell. As this happens, the room starts to spin before your eyes. If you possess the Headband of Concentration, turn to **158**. If you do not, turn to **11**.

### 343

You put the Gold Piece on top of the signpost as requested by the crow, after which it says, 'Go north.' You ask the crow why it needs Gold Pieces and it replies that it needs 30 Gold Pieces to pay Yaztromo to turn it back into a human again. You bid the crow farewell. If you want to turn north as advised by the crow, turn to **8**. If you would rather continue eastwards, turn to **239**.

### 344

You wedge your sword between the jaws of the snare and pull on it like a lever. The robed stranger adds his strength and finally the snare springs open. He thanks you over and over again and explains that he is in the forest looking for his long lost brother, who he thinks is living the life of a hermit somewhere in its depths. Together you scramble back over the roots of the trees to the path. You ask him to accompany you north but he politely declines saying that he believes his brother lives to the south. You shake hands and bid each other farewell. Turn to **36**.

### 345

The pain in your stomach intensifies and sweat breaks out on your forehead. You start to shake. Lose 4 STAMINA points. If you are still alive, the pain gradually fades away. There does not seem to be much sense in staying here any longer and you walk over to the steps on the far wall. Turn to **293**.

### 346

Arragon raises his right arm and spreads the fingers on his hand, saying, 'Well, stranger, what is your decision?' If you wish to give Arragon what he requires, turn to **32**. If you wish to ignore his threat and draw your sword, turn to **111**.

### 347

The Dwarf is a hardy old fighter and swings his axe with great skill.

DWARF          SKILL 8          STAMINA 5

If you win, turn to **363**.

### 348

The men are jumping up and down with their arms in the air in fits of glee as they see you struggling to pull the arrow from your shoulder. You grit your teeth and tug on the arrow; finally it comes free. The men are both laughing out loud, uncontrollably. They seem to forget about you. If you want to attack the WILD HILL MEN, turn to **43**. If you want to walk past them along the path while they continue to laugh, turn to **188**.

**351** *The floor is thick with dust and there are cobwebs everywhere.*

## 349

You arrive back at the crossroads. Ignoring the way south back to the forest you may go north (turn to **291**) or continue east (turn to **102**).

## 350

You reach into your backpack and pull out a small cloth pouch containing the capsules. There are five of them, all shiny red. You take one out and throw it towards the advancing Treeman. It lands in front of him and explodes in a puff of white smoke. A jet of flame shoots up from out of the ground and forces the Treeman to back away. You seize your opportunity and throw the remaining capsules at the Treeman. Flames burst out all around him and you run past him while he is trapped. Soon you are well away from the Treeman and stop running. Heading north you notice that the trees are at last starting to thin out – turn to **329**.

## 351

You step carefully down the stone stairs, feeling your way as you go. Slowly your eyes become accustomed to the dark and you begin to make out shapes at the bottom of the stairs. You are standing in a small, square room with a low ceiling. The floor is thick with dust and there are cobwebs everywhere. In the middle of the room there is what appears to be a large stone box, measuring approximately two metres by one metre. The top of it is a great stone slab. Along one of the rough stone walls you find a small alcove with a candle in it. You may either light the candle (turn to **292**) or walk back up the stairs, return to the path and head north; turn to **112**.

## 352

The Ape Man is very agile around the tree, and you have difficulty brandishing your sword. You must deduct 2 from your Attack Strength during each round of combat.

APE MAN             SKILL 8             STAMINA 7

If you win, turn to **207**. You may *Escape* by jumping off the platform to the ground five metres below. Turn to **156**.

## 353

When you awake you find that you are lying on the ground outside the wooden hut. You sit up and look inside your backpack. All your Provisions have been stolen! Luckily nothing else is gone and you still have your sword. You look inside the hut but it is deserted. If you wish to search the hut for something useful, turn to **26**. If you would rather leave the hut, return to the path and head north, turn to **220**.

## 354

Quin shakes his head in disbelief. He stands up and walks silently to a wooden chest at the back of the hut. He lifts the lid and pulls out a small glass phial. He hands it to you and walks back to the table where he slumps in his chair looking thoroughly dejected.

The dust in the phial sparkles in the light and you put it into your backpack and leave the hut. Outside you walk back to the junction in the path. Turn to **349**.

### 355

You arrive at another junction in the path. Ignoring the way south, you continue east – turn to **340**.

### 356

Stuffed inside the Forest Giant's clothing you find a brass lantern with a green wick. There is no liquid inside it to burn. Perhaps it is a magic lantern. You may:

| | |
|---|---|
| Rub the lantern and make a wish | Turn to **34** |
| Try to light the wick | Turn to **395** |
| Throw the lamp away and head north | Turn to **231** |

### 357

As you walk west along the twisting path you pass another branch leading south to the valley. You ignore it and press on west. Eventually the path ends at a junction. Again, ignoring the way south to the valley, you turn north – turn to **306**.

### 358

Walking along the path, you do not notice a rope noose hidden beneath some fallen leaves ahead of you. Your foot catches in the noose and suddenly you are hauled into the air by the rope which is tied

**360** *The young woman steps forward and tells you that you are trespassing.*

to a sprung tree. In a second you are hanging upside down, suspended by your trapped foot. *Test your Luck*. If you are Lucky, your sword remains in its scabbard, and you are able to use it to cut yourself down from the man trap. Turn to **40**. If you are Unlucky, your sword slips from its scabbard and drops to the ground, leaving you dangling helplessly. Turn to **218**.

### 359

To the left of the path you see a stone well with a bucket and turning handle. If you wish to take a closer look at the well, turn to **172**. If you would rather continue your walk east, turn to **281**.

### 360

Walking along the narrow path you suddenly hear the sharp crack of a twig breaking and the whispering of low voices. You draw your sword and wait anxiously with your back to a large oak tree. Then from behind the trees opposite you step four men and a woman dressed in green tunics. Each looks menacing and they stand with swords and axes in their hands. The young woman steps forward and tells you that you are trespassing on their territory and you must pay a levy of five objects from your backpack or face the consequences. If you wish to give them what they want, turn to **279**. If you would rather spit on the ground in reply and fight them, turn to **104**.

**361**

From not too far ahead comes the sharp noise of barking dogs drawing nearer. Suddenly a brown fox with eyes wide open in fear dashes past you running east. The frantic yelping of the dogs gets louder. If you wish to face the oncoming pack of dogs, turn to **396**. If you would rather hide in the tall grasses off the path and let them run past in pursuit of the fox, turn to **86**.

**362**

Which way are you heading? If you wish to continue east, turn to **281**. If you wish to continue west, turn to **238**.

**363**

You rummage through the Dwarf's backpack and find a corked bottle containing a clear liquid. If you wish to drink the contents of the bottle, turn to **68**. If you would rather leave the bottle and set off east again along the path, turn to **59**.

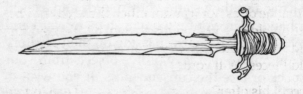

**364**

You nod your head at the masked rider and bid him good-day. He nods back but says nothing. You tell him of your quest to help the dwarfs of

Stonebridge; he then jumps down from his mount, throws back his cape and extends his right arm to shake your hand. You see that each of his fingers is adorned by a large gold ring. Will you:

| | |
|---|---|
| Attack him for his gold? | Turn to **276** |
| Carry on the conversation? | Turn to **194** |

### 365

The gas is toxic and your eyes start to water. You hold your breath long enough to find the Nose Filters and slip them into place inside your nostrils. You inhale tentatively, but all is well. After a while, the gas cloud around your face fades away. You put the silver box into your backpack and leave the cave to continue your quest northwards. Turn to **358**.

### 366

You bid the Centaur good-day, to which he replies in a similar manner. It is pleasing to meet somebody who is not attacking you on sight! You ask the Centaur if he has any information which might lead you to your goal but he does not know anything. He says that he does not wander much these days as he is getting old. He just wants to own a little gold for his old age. He offers to carry you across the river for 3 Gold Pieces. Will you:

| | |
|---|---|
| Accept his offer? | Turn to **127** |
| Refuse politely and wade into the river? | Turn to **178** |

## 367

There is a soft popping sound as the head of the fungus splits open followed by the hiss of escaping gas. You become enveloped by a cloud of poisonous gas. Do you possess Nose Filters? If you do, turn to **60**. If you do not, turn to **222**.

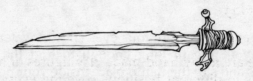

## 368

There is nothing more you can do in this room so you decide to walk back up the stairs and return to the path to head north; turn to **112**.

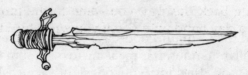

## 369

The valley floor is green and pleasant and you wonder why such a tranquil place should be the home of so many loathsome creatures. Walking along the path, you see in the distance the portly shape of a balding man dressed in long brown robes heading in your direction. As he gets closer you see that he is a friar. Will you:

| | |
|---|---|
| Start a conversation with him? | Turn to **191** |
| Walk past him with a nod of the head? | Turn to **390** |

### 370

You frantically grope about in total darkness. Slowly your vision returns and you stand up again. With your own sight fully restored you set off north again along the path. However, while you were on the ground an item fell out of your backpack. Make the deduction to your Equipment List and turn to **231**.

### 371

There are many hand-made clay figures of human hands in different positions covering every available surface area. They are all painted with bright red glaze. In a copper vase you find 3 Gold Pieces, which you put in your backpack. There is nothing else of use or value to you in the cave. You leave by crawling back the way you came to the junction, taking a clay hand with you if you wish; turn to **93**.

### 372

You bend down and try to lift the chest but it is very heavy. Roll two dice. If the number rolled is less than or equal to your SKILL score, you succeed – turn to **48**. If the number rolled is greater than your SKILL, you injure your back – lose 1 STAMINA point. You may try to lift the chest as many times as you wish by repeating the above procedure. If you succeed, turn to **48**. If you do not manage to lift the chest, you decide not to risk any more injury to your back and leave the room exasperated. Continue north and turn to **288**.

## 373

You slump on to the log exhausted after your long battle. Sadly, the black rod was just part of the Shape Changer's illusion and it exists no more. However, you notice some violet mushrooms growing behind the log. They are unfamiliar to you but look tasty. If you wish to eat some of the mushrooms, turn to **308**. If you would rather continue north, turn to **148**.

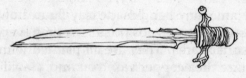

## 374

You slip the gauntlet on to your hand and take hold of your sword. Slicing the air with it you feel more than usually skilled with your weapon. You now possess a Gauntlet of Weapon Skill which will allow you to add 1 point to all future dice rolls when computing your own Attack Strength during combat so long as you wear it. Note this on your Equipment List. If you wish to try on the gold ring, turn to **133**. If you would rather ignore the gold ring (or have already tried it on) you must head north again along the path – turn to **360**.

## 375

A junction appears in the path. If you wish to continue north, turn to **150**. If you wish to head west, turn to **236**.

## 376

*Test your Luck*. If you are Lucky, he does not wake up – turn to **74**. If you are Unlucky, you kick a small stone which rattles across the cave floor and awakens the Cave Troll – turn to **310**.

## 377

You quickly catch up with the two brown-skinned Pygmies. They are wearing grass skirts and as they stop and turn to face you, you notice that each has a small bone through his nose. They draw their daggers and both attack you at once. Both will have a separate attack on you in each Attack Round, but you must choose which of the two you will fight. Attack your chosen Pygmy as a normal battle. Against the other you will throw for your Attack Strength in the normal way, but you will not wound it if your Attack Strength is the greater; you must just count this as though you have fought off its blow. Of course if its Attack Strength is greater, it has wounded you in the normal way.

|  | SKILL | STAMINA |
|---|---|---|
| PYGMY A | 5 | 5 |
| PYGMY B | 5 | 6 |

If you win, turn to **205**. If you wish to *Escape*, run back to the path and turn north. Turn to **92**.

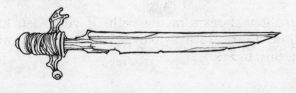

**378** *A small man with a long grey beard is sitting cross-legged on top of a large mushroom.*

## 378

To the left of the path you see a small man with a long grey beard sitting cross-legged on top of a huge mushroom. He is wearing a bright red jacket and cap, and his trousers are black and end at his knees. He is asleep and is snoring loudly. You may either give him a gentle push to wake him up (turn to 307) or walk quietly past him to continue your journey west (turn to 67).

## 379

You may either try to charge the door down (turn to 73) or return to the path and head north (turn to 112).

## 380

If you wish to risk jumping down the hollow tree trunk to the bottom of the tunnel below, turn to 237. If you wish to return to the path to head north again, turn to 144.

## 381

You have failed in your quest to help the dwarfs. Being unable to face Gillibran, their king, you decide to head east and find a place to rest after your perilous adventure. Perhaps you may try again? If you do, you must walk around Darkwood Forest back to Yaztromo's tower to purchase more of his magical items – turn to 98.

**384** *A huge man with muscles like knotted iron is staked to the ground.*

## 382

Going west, the path soon brings you to another junction. You decide to ignore the way south and head north. Turn to 97.

## 383

You search through the bags and clothes of the Orcs and find 2 Gold Pieces and a small wooden whistle. Add these to your Equipment List if you wish. You may also eat the spit-roast rabbit and add 2 points to your STAMINA. Suitably refreshed you return to the path and head north. Turn to 254.

## 384

Ahead in the grasses you hear a low moan. You look up to see the vultures patiently waiting overhead. A few steps further and you see the ugly sight of a huge man with muscles like knotted iron staked out to the ground. His arms and legs are tied to four large wooden pegs driven deep into the ground. The man is naked except for a small loin cloth and his skin is badly blistered from the sun. His face and chest show the bloodied signs of cruel torture. His captors will not have gained the information they sought from him because he is a BARBARIAN! If you wish to cut him free, turn to 128. If you want to leave him in his agony and return to the path to head north, turn to 394.

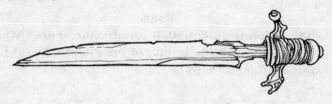

## 385

As the Ogre slumps to the ground, the creature in the cage jumps around even more frantically than before. Do you:

| | |
|---|---|
| Take a closer look at the creature in the cage? | Turn to **168** |
| Search through the contents of the cave? | Turn to **313** |
| Leave the cave immediately and continue northwards? | Turn to **358** |

## 386

You settle down to sleep again but have a restless night. In the morning you wake early. You collect your belongings and set off north along the path. Turn to **119**.

## 387

On the ground in front of you lies a single Gold Piece. You pick it up and toss it in the air with a flick of your thumb. Then you put it in your pocket. Add 1 LUCK point and turn to **340**.

## 388

If the Werewolf wounded you during combat, turn to **155**. If you did not receive any wounds, add 1 LUCK point and turn to **316**.

## 389

You raise your sword above your head and smash it down on the wooden chest. It splinters into tiny pieces and amongst the broken bits of wood you find 8 Gold Pieces. Add 1 LUCK point. If you haven't done so already, you may look in the barrel (turn to **215**) or you may leave the alcove to climb further up the steps (turn to **88**).

## 390

In the distance you see the dark brown wall of trees looming up before you. The path leads directly into Darkwood Forest and soon starts to twist and turn between tangled roots and bushes. The path eventually splits. If you wish to continue north, turn to **190**. If you wish to head west, turn to **280**.

### 391

The building measures only three metres by three metres and has no windows. The door is made of stone and looks very solid. There is no handle and there does not appear that there is another way to enter the building. Then you notice a tiny keyhole in the stone door. Do you possess a silver key? If you do, turn to **200**. If not, turn to **379**.

### 392

As you crouch in the bushes off the path, the voices get louder. Then two pairs of spindly legs in tattered cloth shuffle past you quickly, kicking up dirt and dust. The voices soon fade away into the distance. You step out on to the path again and press on northwards. Turn to **157**.

### 393

Leading along the quiet valley floor, the path comes to an end at a junction. The way south leads back into the hills so you decide against it and head north; turn to **369**.

## 394

Gradually the grass around you becomes shorter as the ground gently starts to rise. Ahead you can hear the sound of flowing water. Soon you reach the bank of a slow-flowing river. The river is very shallow and stepping stones cross it to the far bank where the path continues north into the distance. Will you:

| | |
|---|---|
| Cross the river by the stepping stones? | Turn to **66** |
| Wade through the shallow water across the river? | Turn to **186** |

## 395

Instead of the wick igniting, a blinding flash comes from the lantern, so bright that you are unable to see. You stumble and fall to the ground. *Test your Luck*. If you are Lucky, you land without injury; turn to **154**. If you are Unlucky, your head smashes on a log – lose 3 STAMINA points. If you are still alive, turn to **370**.

**396** *A masked rider on a white stallion gallops towards you in a cloud of dust.*

### 396

You draw your sword and stand to face the pack of dogs. They come into view in a cloud of dust; galloping behind them is a masked rider wearing a long flowing cloak and riding a white stallion. He blows a horn and the pack of dogs comes to a sudden halt in front of you. There are four of them and you see that they are hunting dogs. The stallion stands motionless behind them with steam blowing from its nostrils in two long jets. The masked man looks at you without speaking. Will you:

Start a conversation with him?        Turn to **364**
Attack the dog nearest to you?        Turn to **96**

### 397

You continue your walk along the valley floor, passing a junction in the path which leads south to the hills. You soon arrive at another junction. Again one of the branches leads south to the hills. If you wish to head north, turn to **163**. If you wish to carry on east, turn to **393**.

### 398

You reach the end of the tunnel and are about to step out on to the ladder on the wall of the well when you hear footsteps above you. Somebody is coming down the ladder. If you wish to reach out in an attempt to grab hold of the first leg that comes into view, turn to **320**. If you would rather wait for the visitor to enter the tunnel, turn to **193**.

## 399

You charge at Yaztromo but only reach the first stair when he lifts his right arm and nonchalantly mumbles a few words. Time seems to stand still amid bright flashes, and your body feels like a bubbling liquid inside. When the turmoil subsides, you know something terrible has happened. The stone stair feels cold on your body and you realize the problems of a life as a frog! Yaztromo bends down and picks you up, saying with a booming voice:

'Well, foolish warrior, enjoy your new life!' With that, he lets out a deafening laugh and nearly drops you. Then he shuffles to the oak door and, opening it, throws you into the tall grasses outside. Your adventure ends here.

## 400

You walk up to the old dwarfs and ask them to take you to Gillibran. They eye you suspiciously but agree to do so, commenting on your wounds and torn clothing. 'You got those in Darkwood Forest I presume,' says one of the dwarfs, pointing at various gashes on your body with his long clay pipe. 'Some people never learn. Adventurers are all the same. I can't see the sense in it myself.'

You walk through the village behind the two dwarfs and are aware of many dwarfish folk watching you. They begin to follow you and a procession builds up behind. There are lots of mutterings and whispers amongst the crowd of dwarfs and expectant looks show on their faces. Soon you arrive at the foot of stone steps leading up to a stone building. Outside the building on an ornate wooden throne sits a small old man with a long beard. He is wearing a crown but looks miserable and holds his head in his hands. You run up the steps, taking the hammer head and handle from your backpack. At the sight of them the old dwarf's eyes light up and he jumps to his feet. Taking them eagerly from you he starts to shout 'My hammer! My hammer! We are saved. Now, my people, we are ready to fight the trolls.'

The whole crowd erupts into cheering, waving their axes and swords in the air. You tell Gillibran of Bigleg's misfortune and why you decided to continue his quest, and of all the monsters you have encountered on your way. Gillibran listens and frowns at the news of Bigleg his faithful servant. Then he opens a drawer in the base of the throne and reaches into it, pulling out a small silver box and a golden winged helmet, and hands them to you. The helmet is worth hundreds of Gold Pieces and you proudly place it on your head. A great roar of approval comes from the crowd. You open the silver box and find dozens of jewels and gems. You put these in your backpack and wave to the happy dwarfs of Stonebridge. Your quest is over and you are now wealthy beyond your wildest dreams.

Complete with the *Sorcery! Spell Book,* each
book can be played either on its own or as
part of the whole epic.

## OUT OF THE PIT

### FIGHTING FANTASY MONSTERS

*Steve Jackson and Ian Livingstone*

From the darkest corners, from the deepest pools and from the dungeons thought only to exist in nightmares come the Fighting Fantasy monsters – the downfall of many a brave warrior. Two hundred and fifty of these loathsome creatures from the wild and dangerous worlds of Fighting Fantasy are collected here – some are old adversaries, many you have yet to meet – each of them described in minute detail. An indispensable guide for Fighting Fantasy adventurers!

## TITAN:

## THE FIGHTING FANTASY WORLD

*Steve Jackson and Ian Livingstone*
### Edited by Marc Gascoigne

You met the monsters in OUT OF THE PIT – now meet the rest of the Fighting Fantasy world! No adventurer should be without this essential guide – it contains everything you need to know, covering the turbulent history of the world, from its creation and early civilizations – through the devastating War of the Wizards – to the present-day wilderness and anarchy where the delicate balance between Good and Chaos could at any moment be overturned . . .

# FIGHTING FANTASY

## Steve Jackson

The world of Fighting Fantasy, peopled by Orcs, dragons, zombies and vampires, has captured the imagination of millions of readers world-wide. Thrilling adventures of sword and sorcery come to life in the Fighting Fantasy Gamebooks, where the reader is the hero, dicing with death and demons in search of villains, treasure or freedom.

Now YOU can create your own Fighting Fantasy adventures and send your friends off on dangerous missions! In this clearly written handbook, Steve Jackson has put together everything you need to become a successful GamesMaster. There are hints on devising challenging combats, monsters to use, tricks and tactics, as well as two mini-adventures complete with GamesMaster's notes for you to start with. The ideal introduction to the fast-growing world of role-playing games, and literally countless adventures.

# THE TROLLTOOTH WARS

## Steve Jackson

It started with an ambush. When Balthus Dire's blood-lusting Hill Goblins mount their raid on the Strongarm caravan, little do they realize what dramatic consequences their actions will have. For that caravan carries Cunnelwort, a mystical herb from Eastern Allansia, destined for none other than the evil sorceror, Zharradan Marr! War – between two forces well-matched for evil – is soon to ensue ... Will Balthus Dire's chaotics of Zharradan Marr's undead prove victorious? The answer is here, in the first Fighting Fantasy novel.